Afloat on the Flood

By

Lawrence J. Leslie

AFLOAT ON THE FLOOD

CHAPTER I

THE EVERGREEN RIVER ON THE RAMPAGE

"What's the latest weather report down at the post office, Max?"

"More rain coming, they say, and everybody is as gloomy as a funeral."

"My stars! the poor old town of Carson is getting a heavy dose this spring, for a fact; nothing but rain, rain, and then some more rain."

"Never was anything to beat it, Bandy-legs, and they say even the oldest inhabitant can't remember when the Evergreen River was at a higher stage than it is right now."

"Here comes our chum, Toby Jucklin, and he looks as if he might be bringing some news with him. Hi! Toby, what's the latest?"

The new arrival, who was somewhat out of breath with hurrying, surveyed the two boys who stood there awaiting his arrival, with an expression of almost comical uneasiness on his face. Truth to tell, whenever Toby became in any way excited, and often when he was perfectly calm, his tongue played him cruel tricks, so that he stuttered, and stumbled fearfully; until suddenly stopping he would draw in a long breath, give a sharp whistle, and having thus obtained a grip on himself often proceeded to speak as intelligibly as any one.

"M-m-mills and s-s-shops all closed down, so's to let w-w-workers have c-c-chance to save their h-h-household goods!" he went on to say in a labored manner.

The boy who had been called Bandy-legs by Max, and whose rather crooked lower limbs were undoubtedly responsible for the nickname among his school fellows, gave a whistle to indicate the depth of his feelings.

Toby may have had an obstruction in his vocal cords, but he could run like a streak; on the other hand, while Bandy-legs could not be said to have an elegant walk, which some hateful fellows compared to the waddle of a duck, there was nothing the matter with his command of language, for he could rattle on like the machinery in one of Carson's mills.

"And," he went on to say, excitedly, "the last news I heard was that school would have to stay closed all of next week, because the water is on the campus now, and likely to get in the cellars before the river goes down again. Which means we'll have a week's vacation we didn't count on."

Somehow even that important event, which at another time would have caused the boys to throw their hats into the air with glee, did not seem to create a ripple of applause among the three young chaps. Carson was threatened with a terrible disaster, the greatest in all her history, and even these boys could experience something of the sensation of awe that had begun to pass through the whole community.

The Evergreen River that ran past the town was already bank-full; and all manner of terrifying reports kept circulating among the panic-stricken people of that section of the State, adding to their alarm and uneasiness. More rain meant accessions to the flood, already augmented by the melting of vast quantities of snow up in the mountains, owing to the sudden coming of Spring. Besides this, some people claimed to know that the great reservoir which supplied water to many towns, was not as secure as it might be, and they spread reports of cracks discovered that might suddenly bring about another Johnstown disaster.

It was a strange spectacle that the three boy friends looked upon as they stood on the street corner that Saturday morning. Water had already invaded many of the buildings in the lower section of the town, and in every direction could be seen excited families moving their household goods to higher levels.

Horses and wagons were at a premium that morning, and from the way things looked just then it might not be long before every boat that was owned within five miles would be needed to rescue people imprisoned in their homes, or to carry valuable goods out of the reach of the terrible flood.

The three young fellows whom we meet on this dark morning in the history of the enterprising little town of Carson were chums who had for many moons been accustomed to spending their vacations together in the woods, or on the waters. In all they were five close friends, but Owen Hastings, a cousin of Max, and who had made his home with him, was at present away in Europe with another uncle; and Steve Dowdy happened to be somewhere else in town, perhaps helping his father remove his stock of groceries from his big store, which being in the lower part of town was apt to suffer from the rising waters.

In previous volumes of this series we have followed the fortunes of these chums with considerable pleasure; and those who have been fortunate enough to have read one or more of these stories will need no further introduction to the trio. But while they may have passed through numerous exciting episodes in the days that were gone, the outlook that faced them now seemed to promise even more thrilling adventures.

No wonder all of them showed signs of excitement, when all around them men and women were moving swiftly to gather up their possessions, or standing in groups watching the swiftly passing flood, if their homes chanced to be safely out of reach of the river's utmost grip.

A heavy wooden bridge crossed the river at Carson. This had withstood the floods of many previous Springs, but it was getting rather old and shaky, and predictions were circulating that there was danger of its being carried away, sooner or later, so that the more timid people kept aloof from it now.

The four chums had only a short time before returned from an Eastern camping trip up amidst the hills about fifteen miles from town. They had experienced some strange adventures while in camp, most of which hinged upon an event that had taken place in Carson one windy night, when the big round-top of a visiting circus blew down in a sudden gale, and many of the menagerie animals were set free.

At the time of their home-coming the boys had certainly never anticipated that there would be a renewal of activity in such a short time. Why, it seemed that they had hardly become settled again at their studies when the rapid rising of the Evergreen River on Friday night brought the town of Carson face to face with a threatened disaster that might yet be appalling.

"Does anybody know where Steve is?" asked Max, when they had been observing the remarkable sights that were taking place all around them for some little time, now laughing at some comical spectacle, and again springing to help a little girl who was staggering under a heavy load, or a woman who needed assistance, for all of them had generous hearts.

"He told me early this morning that his father had a dozen hands employed carrying the stuff up out of the basement of the grocery store and taking it to the second story," Bandy-legs replied.

"I wish I'd known that," remarked Max; "for I'd have offered to help, because my house happens to be well up on the highest ground in town, and nothing could hurt us, even if the reservoir did burst, which I surely hope it won't."

They exchanged uneasy glances when Max mentioned the possibility of that disaster coming upon the unhappy valley, which would suffer seriously enough from the flood without that appalling happening coming to pass.

"D-d-don't mention it, Max, p-p-please," said Toby, with a gloomy shake of his head; "because while my f-f-folks might be out of d-d-danger from a regular f-f-flood, if a monster wave of water came a s-s-sweepin' along down here, it'd sure ketch us, and make our p-p-place look like a howling wilderness."

"Same with me," added the third boy; "but I don't believe that reservoir's goin' to play hob with things, like some people say. They're shaking in their shoes right now about it; but if the new rain that's aheadin' this way'd only get switched off the track I reckon we'd manage to pull through here in Carson without a terrible loss. I'd say go down and help Mr. Dowdy, Max, but I just heard a man tell that everything in the cellar had been moved, and they were cleaning out the lower floor so's not to take chances."

"But we might get around and see if we couldn't help somebody move," suggested Max; "it would be only play for us, but would mean a whole lot to them."

"S-s-second the motion," assented Toby, quickly. "And say, fellows, I was just thinking about that poor widow, Mrs. Badger, and her t-t-three children. Her house is on low g-g-ground, ain't it; and the water must be around the d-d-doorsill right now. G-g-give the word, Max, and let's s-s-scoot around there to see."

Max was the acknowledged leader of the chums, and as a rule the others looked to him to take command whenever any move was contemplated.

"That was a bright thought of yours, Toby," he now said, as he shot a look full of boyish affection toward his stuttering chum; "if you do get balled up in your speech sometimes, there's nothing the matter with your heart, which is as big as a bushel basket. So come on, boys, and we'll take a turn around that way to see what three pair of willing hands can find to do for the widow and her flock."

They had to make a little circuit because the water was coming up further in some of the town streets all the tune, with a rather swift current that threatened to undermine the foundations of numerous flimsy buildings, if the flood lasted long.

"Whew! just look out there at the river, would you?" exclaimed Bandy-legs, when they came to a spot where an unobstructed view could be obtained of the yellow flood that was whirling past the town at the rate of many miles an hour, carrying all sorts of strange objects on its bosom, from trees and logs, to hencoops and fence rails.

They stood for a minute or so to gaze with ever increasing interest at the unusual spectacle. Then as the three boys once more started to make their tortuous way along, avoiding all manner of obstacles, Max went on to say:

"Pretty hard to believe that's our old friend the Evergreen River, generally so clear and pretty in the summer time, and with such good fishing in places up near where the Big Sunflower and the Elder branches join. And to think how many times we've skated for twenty miles up and down in winter; yet look there now, and you'd almost believe it was the big Mississippi flowing past."

"And mebbe you noticed," observed Toby, warmly, "how f-f-funny the b-b-bridge looks with the w-w-water so near the s-s-span. Let me tell you, if ever she does g-g-get up so's to wash the roadway, g-g-good-bye to b-b-bridge. I wouldn't want to be on it right then."

"Nor me, either," Max added; "but that bridge has weathered a whole lot of floods, and let's hope it won't go out this time either; though we do need a new one the worst kind. But here's the widow's place, boys, and seems like she does need help. The water's creeping up close to her door, and inside another hour it would be all over the floors of her cottage. There she is, looking out now, and with three kids hanging to her dress. Let's ask her where we could take her stuff near by. She hasn't got so much but that we might save most of it."

The poor woman looked white and frightened, and indeed there was reason she should with that flood closing in on her little home and her helpless family. When the three chums proposed to carry the best of her belongings to higher ground she thanked them many times. It happened that she had a friend whose home was not far away, and on a good elevation; so anything that could be taken there she might have stored in their barn, where doubtless the friend would allow her to stay temporarily, until the river receded.

Accordingly the stout boys settled down to business, and were soon staggering under heavy loads, just as many other people in Carson chanced to be doing at that time. It was slow and laborious work, and Max knew that they would never be able to get some of the heavier articles to a place of safety. Although they did not represent any great commercial value, still they were all in all to Mrs. Badger.

Just then an idea came into his head which he hastened to put into execution. An empty wagon was passing, and Max recognized it as belonging to his father. Mr. Hastings, realizing the need of all the conveyances that could be obtained, had sent his man down town with the conveyance, so as to be of assistance to those in distress.

Calling to the man Max soon had him backing up to the cottage, and the heavier things, such as the cook stove, beds, wash tubs and other household articles were soon loaded. In this fashion the possessions of the widow were saved from being water soaked, for before they had taken the last thing out the river was lapping her doorstep greedily, and steadily rising all the while.

Having dismissed the driver with his wagon, to go and make himself useful elsewhere, Max and his two chums were walking slowly along, wondering what next they might do, when a fourth boy was seen hurrying toward them.

"There comes Steve," announced Bandy-legs, whose quick eyesight had discovered the approach of the other chum, "and chances are he's bringing some news, because he carries the map on his face. 'Touch-and-Go Steve' we call him, because he's ready to fly off his base at the first crack of the gun; but he's sure got plenty now to excite him. Hello! Steve, how's things getting on at the store?"

"Oh! my dad's got his stock out of reach of the water, all that could be hurt by a soaking; and he thinks the brick building will stand if the reservoir don't give way; but did you hear that the river is above the danger line by two feet; higher than ever before known, and rising like a race-horse all the time? Gee whiz! what's the answer to this question; where's this thing going to end?" and Steve looked at his three chums as he put this question; but they only shook their heads in reply, and stared dolefully out on the swiftly rushing river.

CHAPTER II

LENDING A HELPING HAND

"What we see here isn't all of the trouble by a lot," Max ventured, as they stood and watched the remarkable sights all around them.

"I should say not," Steve quickly added; "already they've begun to get reports of washouts down below, where houses have left their foundations, and gone off on the current; while barns, chicken coops, pig pens and fences are being swept away by dozens and scores. It's going to be the most terrible flood that ever visited this section. I only hope nobody gets drowned in it, that's all."

"I met Gus French a while back," Bandy-legs happened to remember, though he had said nothing of the circumstance before, there being so many exciting events taking place right along, "and he told me they were a heap worried at their house."

"What for?" demanded Steve, who had a weakness for the pretty sister of Gus, though of late there had existed a foolish coolness between them, founded on some small happening that grew into a misunderstanding; "their house stands higher than a whole lot in town, and I don't see why they'd worry."

"Oh! it ain't that," the other boy hastened to say; "but p'raps you didn't know that yesterday Mazie Dunkirk and Bessie French went to stay over Sunday with an aunt of the French girl's about twenty miles down the river; and they say that the old house is on pretty low ground, so that if the river rises much more she might be carried off the foundation!"

Steve gave a half groan, and Max too turned a little white, for the Mazie whom Bandy-legs referred to was a very good friend of his, whom he had always escorted to barn dances and singing school, and also skated with winters.

"If I had a friend who owned a good motorboat now," said Steve, between his set teeth, "I give you my word I'd like to borrow the same."

"W-w-what for?" demanded Toby, appalled at the thought of any one venturing out on that swirling river in a puny powerboat.

"I'd take chances, and run down below to see if I could be of any help to the folks there," Steve went on to say, gloomily; "but I don't know anybody that I might borrow even a skiff from."

"Yes, and if you did, the chances are he'd think twice before loaning you his boat," Max told him. "In the first place he'd expect you to snag the craft, and sink the same, because you do everything with such a rush and whoop. And then again, the way things look around here every boat that's owned within five miles of town will be needed to rescue people from second-story windows before to-morrow night."

"D-d-do you think it's g-g-going to be as b-b-bad as all that, Max?"

"I'm afraid so, Toby, if half of all that rain gets here, with the river more than out of its banks now. But, Steve, I wouldn't worry about the girls if I were you. Long before this Bessie's relatives have taken the horses, and made for the higher ground of the hills. Even if you did manage to get down there you'd find the house empty, and have all your work for nothing."

Steve did not answer, but his face remained unusually serious for a long time, since he was doubtless picturing all sorts of terrible things happening to the girls who were visiting down the river.

As the morning advanced more and more discouraging reports kept circulating through the stricken town. The river was rising at a rate that promised to cause its waves to lap the roadway of the bridge by night-time; and everybody believed this structure was bound to go out before another dawn.

It was about the middle of the morning when the four chums, in wandering around bent on seeing everything that was going on during such exciting times, came upon a scene that aroused their immediate indignation.

Several rough half-grown young rowdies had pretended to offer to assist a poor old crippled storekeeper remove his stock of candies and cakes from the threatened invasion of the waters, already lapping his door and creeping across the floor of his little shop. Their intentions however were of a far different character, for they had commenced to pounce upon the dainties on his shelves, despite his weak if energetic protests.

"What you shoutin' about, old codger?" demanded one of the three bullies, as he crammed his pockets with whatever he fancied in the line of candy; "the water's coming right in and grab all your stock, anyway; so, what difference does it make if we just lick up a few bites? Mebbe we'll help get the rest of your stuff out of this, if so be we feels like workin'. So close your trap now, and let up on that yawp!"

Max and the others heard this sort of talk as they stopped outside the door of the little candy shop in which, as small lads, they could remember having spent many a spare penny.

It filled them with indignation, first because they thought a good deal of the poor old crippled man who made a scant living selling small toys and candies to the school children; and second on account of the fact that they knew this set of rowdies of old, having had many disputes with them in the past.

Their former leader, Ted Shatter, had been missed from his accustomed haunts for some time now, and it was whispered that he had been sent to a reform school by his father, who wielded considerable power in political circles, but could not expect to keep his lawless boy from arrest if he continued to defy the authorities as he had been doing.

Since then the "gang" had been led by a new recruit, named Ossie Kemp; and the other two with him were the old offenders, who have appeared before now in the stories of this series, Amiel Toots and Shack Beggs.

"Back me up, boys," said Max, hastily turning to his three chums, "and we'll run that crowd out of there in a hurry, or know the reason why."

"We'll stand by you, Max," replied Bandy-legs, quickly.

"You b-b-bet we will," added Toby, aggressively doubling up his fists.

"To the limit!" echoed Steve, stooping down to secure a stout stick his roving eye chanced to alight upon, and which appealed to his fighting instincts as just the thing for an emergency like this.

Max immediately pushed straight into the little store, and, as he expected would be the case, his eyes fell first upon the raiding bullies, and then the slight figure of the distressed crippled storekeeper, wringing his hands as he faced complete ruin, between his inhuman persecutors and the pitiless flood.

At the entrance of a new lot of boys the poor old man gave a cry of despair, as though he believed that this would complete his misfortune; then as he recognized Max Hastings a sudden gleam of renewed hope struggled across his face; for Max had a splendid reputation in Carson, and was looked up to as a fine fellow who would certainly never descend to inflicting pain on a helpless cripple.

"What's going on here?" demanded Max, as the three rowdies turned to face the newcomers, and, made cowardly by guilt, looked ready to sneak away. "We're the advance guard of those coming to help you, Mr. McGirt; what are these boys doing here, and did you tell them to fill their pockets with your stock?"

"No, no, not at all!" cried the storekeeper, in a quivering voice; "they burst in on me and I asked them to please carry some of the stock I've tied up in packages to higher ground, for I shall be ruined if I lose what little I've got; but they just laughed at me, and started to taking whatever they fancied. I would not mind if only they saved my property first, and then treated themselves afterwards."

Max frowned fiercely at the three skulking boys. He had purposely spoken as if there might be men coming on the run to assist old Mr. McGirt; for he knew the aggressive natures of at least Shack and Ossie, though Amiel

Toots was a craven who generally struck behind one's back and then ran off; and Max did not care to engage in any fight at such a time and with such a crew.

"If you don't empty every pocket, and then clear out of here, I'll see that you are accused of robbery; and when there's a flood like this they often hang looters to the lamp-posts, perhaps you know? The people won't stand for anything like that. Hurry and put everything back or I'll see that you land in the lock-up. Steve, be ready to step out and give the signal to the Chief if I tell you to. Turn that other pocket inside-out, Amiel Toots. You did expect to make a fine haul here, didn't you? Instead of helping the poor old man save his stock you thought you might as well have it as the water. Are you all through? Then break away, and good riddance to the lot of you for a pack of cowards and thieves!"

Amiel Toots slunk away with a cowed look; Shack Beggs and Ossie Kemp followed him out of the door, but they were black in the face with rage and fear; and the look they shot at Max showed that should the opportunity ever come to even the score they would only too willingly accept chances in order to wipe the slate clean.

"And now, Mr. McGirt, we're ready to help you any way we can," continued Max, once the three young desperadoes had departed to seek new pastures for exploiting their evil natures; "where could we carry these packages you've got done up? And while we're on our way, perhaps you could get the rest of your stock ready. We'll fetch back the empty baskets."

The poor cripple's peaked face glowed with renewed hope, for he had been hovering on the brink of despair.

"Oh! how glad I am you came when you did," he said, in trembling tones; "I would have lost everything I had in the world, between the water and those young ruffians. One of them even had the audacity to ask me why I had bothered cleaning out my cash drawer. If I could only move my stuff up the hill to Mr. Ben Rollins' print shop I'm almost sure he would find a corner where I could store the packages until the river went down again, for he is a very good friend of mine."

"All right," said Steve, "and we know Mr. Rollins well, too. I've even helped him gather up news for his weekly paper, Town Topics. So load up, fellows, and we'll see what can be done. It wouldn't only take a few trips to carry this lot of stuff up there."

Each boy took all he could carry and started off, while the store-keeper commenced hurriedly packing the balance of his stock in trade into bundles, pleased with the new outlook ahead, and grateful for these young friends who had come so unexpectedly to his assistance in his darkest hour of need.

After all it was hardly more than fun for Max and his comrades, because they were all fairly stout fellows, and accustomed to an active outdoor life. They were back again before the owner of the little shop expected they could have gone half the distance.

"It's all right, sir," Bandy-legs hastened to assure Mr. McGirt; "the editor of the paper happened to be there, hurrying out some handbills warning people to prepare for the worst that might come; and he said you were quite welcome to store your stuff in his shed. He only wished everybody else down in the lower part of town could save their belongings, too; but there's bound to be an awful loss, he says. Now, let's load up again, fellers; I feel that I could stagger along under what I've gathered together here; and this trip ought to pretty well clean things up, hadn't it, Max?"

"I think it will," replied the other, also collecting a load as large as he believed himself able to carry. "And if I can find our man with his wagon, Mr. McGirt, I'll have him take what furniture you've got in that little room back there, and put it with your stock in the print shop."

"Thank you a thousand times, Max," said the old cripple; and somehow those four lads fancied that they had been repaid many times over for what they had done as they saw his wrinkled face lose its look of worry and taken on a smile of fresh hope and gratitude.

It happened that Max did run across their hired man busily engaged in carrying some one's furniture up the hill; and he agreed to look after the cripple the very next thing.

"Be sure you make him ride with you, Conrad," was the last thing Max told the man, who faithfully promised to look after the little old storekeeper, and see that he got to a place of-safety.

It was now getting along toward noon. No sun shone above, indeed, they had seen nothing but a leaden sky for a number of days; which of course added to the gloom that surrounded the unfortunate town, as well as the farms and hamlets strung along the valley through which the Evergreen River flowed.

"Get together again after we've had some lunch!" Steve told his three mates, as they started for their respective homes—rather reluctantly; because so many exciting things seemed to be happening every half hour that none of them wanted to miss any more than they could help. Indeed, it is a question whether anything less serious than satisfying the cravings of hunger, always an important subject with a growing boy, would have induced them to go home at all.

"How high was it the last report?" asked Bandy-legs; for somehow there always seems to be a peculiar fascination about learning the worst, when floods rage, and destruction hovers overhead.

"Two feet, nine inches above the danger line, and still coming up an inch an hour, with another big rain promised soon!" replied Steve, promptly, though he did not seem to take any particular pride in the fact that all previous records had already been broken by the usually peaceful Evergreen stream.

"G-g-gosh!" gasped Toby, "there never was, and never will be again such a fierce time in old Carson. B-b-beats that morning I found all them animals from the c-c-circus a gathered in my back yard where I had my own little m-m-menagerie. S-s-see you later, everybody," and with that he actually started on a run for home, doubtless only thinking that he might in this way shorten the time he would be forced to stay away from the river front, where things were happening it seemed, every minute of the day.

Few regular meals were served in Carson that day. People were too much alarmed over the dismal prospect facing the manufacturing town to think of taking things easy. They stayed on the streets, and gathered in groups, talking about the flood, and trying to find some loophole of hope; but many pale faces could be seen among the women, and there was an increasing demand for wagons to haul household goods from the lower sections to places of safety.

That was certainly a day never to be forgotten in Carson; and what made it even worse was the gloomy outlook which the weather predictions held out to those already in the grip of the greatest flood in the history of the valley.

CHAPTER III

ON THE TREMBLING BRIDGE

Once more the four chums came together at a given point, filled with a desire to see with their own eyes the strange sights that were transpiring continually all around them.

The excitement constantly grew in volume, and everywhere groups of men and women, as well as children, could be seen discussing the latest news, or it might be industriously trying to save their possessions from the greedy river.

Many of the younger generation failed to realize the gravity of the situation. All this bustle was in the nature of a picnic to them. They shouted, and called to one another, as they ran hither and thither, watching the unusual scenes. Many times they had to be warned of the danger they ran when playing close to the swift current that was eddying through the lower streets.

Steve Dowdy was always eager to collect the latest news. He had more than once declared that he meant to be a reporter when he grew up, for he practiced the art of cross-questioning people whenever he had a chance; and Max, who had noticed how well he did this, more than once told him he would make a good lawyer instead.

When he joined the others they fully expected that he would have something new to tell them, nor were they mistaken.

"Last word is that the railroad has gone out of commission," Steve announced.

"In the name of goodness, do you mean it's been washed away, where it runs along the river?" exclaimed Bandy-legs, his face showing more or less dismay.

"Well, I don't know that it's as bad as that," Steve admitted; "but the water's up so deep over the tracks that orders have been given to abandon all trains until there's a change."

"Which I should think would be a wise thing to do," Max remarked; "because they couldn't tell but what they'd run into a gap, and a train be lost. Railroads have troubles enough without taking such risks."

"But what if the river keeps booming along like this for a week?" suggested Bandy-legs, prone to imagine things much worse than they were in truth.

"Not much danger of that," ventured Steve; "but even then why should it matter to us if trains couldn't run?"

"Huh! how long d'ye think the town of Carson could live without grub?" was what the other flung at him. "Every day the visible food supply would keep on getting lower and lower, with everything going out and nothing coming in. And deliver me from running up against a regular famine. A feller has got to eat if he wants to live, don't he?"

"You do, we know that, Bandy-legs, and so does Toby here," jeered Steve; "but it strikes me you forget the farmer community when you talk about our going hungry. A good many might be kept from coming into town with loads, but there'd be enough to keep things moving along. What's the use bothering about that; plenty of other things to keep you guessing. It'd ease my mind a heap for instance if I just knew the girls had left that house of Asa French down below, and taken to higher ground. Can't help thinking they might be foolish enough to try and stay there till the water got so high all around that only a boat could be of any use, and they mightn't have one. I even tried to see if I could borrow a boat of any kind, but you couldn't right now, for love or money. Everybody's holding on to what they've got."

"W-w-well, when it's f-f-flooding like it is now, don't you reckon it's the right thing to keep an ark, if so be you g-g-got one? Where'd old Noah a been if he'd allowed himself to be tempted to b-b-bargain for his b-b-boat when the rain started to come down? Wish I had even a canoe myself; I'd feel easier a h-h-heap, let me tell you."

Toby was beginning to take the thing very seriously. He seldom laughed now, and many of the rather pitiful sights he saw all around him made an indelible impression on his mind.

"Worse luck we can't see all that's coming down the river," ventured Steve, presently. "The water's getting so high that it's hard to find a place where you can look out over the whole valley. And I've fetched my camera along, too, hoping to snatch off a few pictures to remember this flood by. Tell you what, fellows, I've got a good notion to go out on the bridge, and snap off some views."

"Pretty risky!" suggested Max.

"They're warning everybody to keep away from the bridge," added Bandy-legs, as he shook his head dubiously, yet seemed inclined to side with Steve; for like all boys, the spirit of daring and love for adventure lay strong within him.

To the surprise of the others Toby piped up just then in a strain they had not imagined would appeal to him.

"That's what the t-t-timid ones keep on saying," he observed; "but I d-d-don't think the old bridge'll get shaky till the current of the r-r-river really hits up against the roadway hard. Now, mebbe some of you've been awonderin' what made me fetch this coil of new clothes line along, danglin' from my arm? W-w-want to k-k-know?"

"To be sure we do, Toby, so rattle it off, won't you?" said Steve.

"All r-r-right, I will," the accommodating Toby assured him. "Well, you s-s-see, there's so many hencoops afloatin' along seems like there might be a dog or a rooster settin' on top of one, and I thought if I had a chance to get out on the b-b-bridge span I'd try and rope one of the same. I've p-p-practiced throwing a lariat some, and I t-t-think I might snatch somethin' from a watery g-g-grave."

The others laughed at the suggestion. In imagination they could see Toby tossing his noosed rope wildly out over the rushing waters, and only to make many a miss.

At the same time Steve chose to encourage him for reasons of his own. With Bandy-legs hesitating, if only he could get Toby to support his suggestion, there was a pretty good chance that conservative Max would give in to superior numbers.

So Steve commenced to handle his little camera, which he had slung over his shoulder with a stout strap.

"The sun don't shine, but it's pretty light right now at one o'clock," he went on to say, meaningly; "and I'm dead sure I could pick up some dandy pictures of the river, and also of poor old Carson, flood-bound. Bandy-legs, how about you; won't you come along with Toby and me out on the bridge?"

The appeal proved to be the finishing stroke, since Bandy-legs had been balancing on the fence.

"All right, Steve, count on me; and, Max, say you'll go along too, if all the rest of us do," he hastened to say.

Max laughed.

"Do you know what you make me think of, you fellows?" he told them; "well, of the time Steve here went in swimming, when there was even a suspicion of ice along the edge of the pond. I can see him now, up to his neck, nearly frozen stiff with the chill, and his teeth rattling in his head as he tried to grin, and called out to the rest of us: 'Come on in, fellows; the water's fine!' But if my three chums are bent on taking risks with that old bridge, I reckon I'll have to join the procession, and go out there along with you. Besides, I've been thinking that we might have a chance to do some rescue work, because any old time somebody is apt to come down the swollen river hanging to a floating log or a frame house. I'm surprised that it hasn't happened before now."

"Well, come on, and don't let's stand around here talking so long," Steve urged, for he was nearly always in a great hurry, which fact had been the main cause for his school mates dubbing him "Touch-and-Go-Steve."

As the four boys approached the bridge they must have felt more or less qualms of nervous apprehension, because the prospect was appalling, with the river up only a comparatively few feet below the centre of the span. But each hesitated to let his companions see that he felt timid in the least; and assuming a carelessness that he was far from feeling, Steve was the first to set foot on the approach to the bridge that spanned the Evergreen River.

Several men called out to warn them that it was dangerous, but no one really attempted to stop them from walking out. As the water was already commencing to lap the roadway at the end, they had to pick their steps; but once out toward the middle it seemed as though confidence began to return.

Pride kept all of the boys from allowing anything like a tremor to appear in their voices when they exchanged remarks. At the same time all of them felt the quivering of the structure, and could understand what a mighty force was commencing to pluck at its supports. When these were undermined, if such a thing should happen, the whole affair would go with a rush, and they realized what that would mean.

Steve immediately busied himself in snapping off several pictures, posing his chums so that they would enter into his views of the flood as seen from the river bridge. In this interesting work he forgot the peril he was running; while Max and Toby and Bandy-legs found plenty to do in looking all around, and watching the strange spectacle of floating trees or logs wedge up against the bridge at various places until they began to form quite a barricade.

"That's what will tell against the bridge more than anything else," Max remarked, as he pointed to where a tree was being pressed by the rush of the water, so that it kept striking against the abutment on the side toward Carson. "When a certain quantity of floating stuff begins to exert all its push against the bridge it'll have to go. We've got to keep our eyes open, boys, and be ready to skip out of here if we see another big tree coming down."

"There's another hencoop, and, Toby, what do I see on the bridge but a big Plymouth Rock rooster!" exclaimed Bandy-legs, excitedly, "so Johnny get your gun, or else your rope, and let's see what sort of a cowboy you c'n be."

Toby ran along the upper side of the bridge, and with his rope coiled awaited a chance to let fly. The conditions were not as favorable as he might have liked, for the railing seemed to be somewhat in the way; and an object moving swiftly toward him did not offer any great hope for his success in casting the lariat; but when the proper time had arrived he bravely let fly.

"Whoop! see it drop right over the old rooster would you?" yelled Bandy-legs; "pull as quick as you can, Toby! Aw! you're slow as molasses in winter, and it just slipped over his back. And now he's running under the bridge, and you won't have fricasseed chicken for supper to-night, as you expected."

"B-b-but you all saw how I d-d-dropped the n-n-noose right over him, didn't you? And that c-c-counts some. When I g-g-get the hang of the thing I expect to do a heap b-b-better. Watch out for another hencoop, Bandy-legs, that's a good feller. I'm sure enjoying myself first-rate."

"Well, looks to me like something coming along up there again," remarked Bandy-legs, who had splendid eyesight, and was sometimes called "Eagle Eye" by his comrades.

"A dog this time, seems like," suggested Steve, carelessly. "I wonder now if I could get his picture when he comes closer? It'd be worth keeping, just to show what sort of things you'll meet up with when there's a big flood on. I reckon I'll try it anyhow; no damage done if I make a foozle."

He hunted up a suitable place, where he thought the light would be most serviceable, and then started to focus his camera on a spot which he selected; when the drifting piece of wreckage reached that position it would be at the proper distance for effective work, and he could press the button with the belief that he had obtained a good picture.

Max was intently looking up the river.

All these things interested him, naturally, though deep down in his heart he knew that they were taking big risks in remaining out on the bridge when others more sensible or less adventurous carefully refrained from trusting themselves to view the flood from so dangerous a standpoint.

The three other boys heard Max give utterance to a startled exclamation. It was not his nature to betray excitement unless there was some very good excuse for doing so, and consequently Steve turned his head to look over his shoulder and ask: "What ails you, Max, old chum? The shaking didn't feel any worse, did if? I'd hate some myself to go with the old bridge, if she does take a notion to cut loose from her moorings, and head down the valley; and, Max, if you reckon we'd better quit this monkey business, and go ashore, why, I'll call it off, though I did want to get this one picture the worst kind."

"Wait!" said Max, quickly; "we couldn't go now, no matter how much we wanted to!"

"Oh! why not?" exclaimed Bandy-legs, looking anxious, as he fancied he felt a new and sickening swaying to the bridge; and unconsciously he gripped the railing while speaking, as though desirous of having something substantial to hold on to.

"Because, unless I'm away off in my guess," said Max, positively, "that object on that roof of a cabin you thought was a dog is a little child; and we've got to try our level best to save it when the wreckage gets down to the bridge!"

His words almost stunned the others. They stood and gazed at the swiftly approaching floating object as though unable to believe their very eyes; but soon Steve managed to find his voice, for he bellowed:

"Max, it is, for a fact, a poor little abandoned child, crouching there, and like as not nearly frightened out of its life. Oh! I wonder what's become of its mother and father? P'raps they've been drowned. Max, what can we do to save it? Think as fast as ever you did in all your life. I'd never get over it if we let that helpless child sweep under the bridge like that rooster did. It'd haunt me the rest of my days. Max, haven't you thought up a plan?"

"Yes, and it's the only way we can have a chance," replied the other, quickly. "Here, let me have the noose end of your rope, Toby; I'm going to slip it around under my arms. Then you three get hold, and I'll climb over the railing here, just where that cabin roof is going to pass under. Too bad that there's so much room, because it won't stick fast; so I must drop down on the roof and grab the child. Everything depends on how you can get me up again. It's all got to be done like a flash, you see. And if the rope holds, I'll do my part, I promise you."

"Count on us, Max, and here's hoping you do get hold of the poor little thing!" said Steve, who had laid his camera aside, the better to use both hands.

They nerved themselves for the coming ordeal. Teeth were tightly clenched, and every muscle summoned to do its full duty. Nor could the emergency be long delayed, because that drifting wreckage of a cabin was approaching them swiftly, borne on the wild current of the flood, and in another ten seconds would have reached the middle of the span of the bridge!

CHAPTER IV

A BRAVE RESCUE

They could hear shouting on the shore, though not daring to pay any attention to it just then, lest it distract their minds from the dangerous business they had on hand.

No doubt some one had discovered that a little child was coming floating down on the swollen current of the river, and the startling news was being communicated from mouth to mouth with the astonishing celerity with which such things can travel.

Had the boys but glanced toward the bank they would have seen people running madly to and fro, and gathering in larger clusters than ever wherever they could get a chance to see out upon the raging waters.

Max had calculated things carefully. He did not want to make any mistake when he clambered over the railing, because such a thing might be fatal to whatever hope he had of rescuing the child.

They could now see plainly that it was a little boy. He was clinging to some part of the surging roof, which seemed to be in danger of capsizing at any moment, for it wobbled fearfully. Max prayed that it would hold its own until he had been given a chance to do his part. He also hoped that he would have sufficient strength in his arms to snatch the child, and then hold him, while his chums tugged and pulled to get them both safely up to the bridge.

As he watched the coming of the fragment of a roof, he was doing some nice calculating, making up his mind just how he must seize upon the one he wished to save, and allow nothing to keep him from obtaining full possession. He had feared that the child might have been tied there by his mother, and had such proven to be the case a rescue must have been well nigh hopeless; but the closer the onrushing object came the more Max assured himself that there did not seem to be any obstacle to his success.

He was over the rail now. Those on shore must have seen what the boy meant to try and accomplish, for all of a sudden a terrible hush had fallen on the gathered groups. Every eye was doubtless glued on the figure that clung to the rail out there, over the rushing waters, waiting for the proper second to arrive. Women unconsciously hugged their own little ones all the tighter to their breasts, perhaps sending up sincere thanks that it was not their child in peril; and at the same time mute prayers must have gone out from many hearts that the brave boy succeed in his mission.

"Steady, Max, old pal!" said Steve, who was braced there for the expected strain. "Don't worry about us, for we'll back you up. Get a clutch on him, and the rest is going to be easy. Ready now!"

Max heard all this but was paying no attention to what was being said. His whole mind was concentrated on the swaying roof of the wrecked cabin, and the piteous sight of that frightened little fellow clinging desperately there.

He could not depend on anything his chums might decide, but must himself judge of the proper time to drop down. The swiftness of the current had to be taken into consideration, as well as the swaying of the wreckage.

When he felt sure of himself Max suddenly let go his precarious hold on the lower part of the railing. It was a bold thing to do, and must have sent a shudder through many a breast ashore, as men and women held their breath, and stared at the thrilling spectacle.

Fortunately Max Hastings was no ordinary lad. He not only had a faculty for laying out plans, but the ability to execute the same as well. And besides that, his love of outdoor life had given him such a muscular development that athletic feats were possible with him such as would have proven rank failures with many other boys.

His judgment proved accurate, for he dropped exactly upon the fragment of the cabin roof, and directly in front of the crouching child. The little fellow must have been watching him, for instantly two hands were outstretched toward Max as though some intuition told the child that his only hope of escape from the angry flood lay in the coming of this boy.

Like a flash Max swooped down upon him. His movements were wonderfully quick, because he knew that this was absolutely necessary when coping with such a treacherous enemy as that moving flood.

He snatched the child up in one arm and held him almost fiercely to his breast. If the little fellow gave utterance to any sort of cry Max failed to hear it, though that in itself might not be so very strange, for there were all sorts of roaring sounds in his ears just then.

Almost at the same instant he felt himself roughly plucked off his feet, and being swung upward. His comrades were tugging at the rope savagely, knowing that unless they were very speedy Max would find himself engulfed in the waters; and the work of rescue be made doubly difficult.

The rope proved equal to the terrific strain, thanks to Toby's good judgment when selecting a braided line with which to play the role of cow puncher and lariat thrower.

Max felt the water around his legs, but that was all, for he did not go down any further than his knees; and yet the suction was tremendous even at that.

He was now being slowly but surely drawn upward, and this was a task that called for the united powers of the three who had hold of the rope. Bandy-legs had been wise enough to wrap the end around a beam that projected from the flooring of the bridge. He did not know what might happen, and was determined that Max should not be swept away on the flood, if it came to the worst.

When they had drawn their comrade far enough up so that Steve, calling on the others to hold fast, bent down and took the child from the grasp of Max, it was an easy matter for the latter to clamber over the rail himself.

Steve was already holding the rescued child up so that those on shore could see that the attempt at rescue had met with a glorious success; for he was naturally proud of his chum's work.

A deep-throated hum broke out; it was the sound of human voices gathering force; and then a wild salvo of cheers told that the good people of Carson could appreciate a brave deed when they saw it, no matter if disaster did hover over the town, and kept them shivering with a dread of what was coming next.

Some of the more impetuous would have started to rush out on the bridge, in order to tell Max what they thought of him; only that several cool-headed men kept these impulsive ones back.

"Keep off!" they kept shouting, waving the crowd away; "if you rushed out there now it would be the last straw to send the bridge loose from its moorings. Stay where you are, men, women! You would only invite a terrible tragedy by going on the bridge!"

"Bring the child to us, boys!" some of the men shouted, waving to the little group out there; since the mountain was not to be allowed to come to Mahomet, Mahomet must go to the mountain.

"Take him across, Max!" said Bandy-legs. "Steve, you take him!" urged Max, not wishing to be lionized, because he happened to be an unusually modest lad, and it bothered him to have men and women wanting to shake him by the hand, telling him how brave he was, and all that.

Steve wanted to protest, but he could see that his chum really meant it, and did not intend to allow himself to be made a hero of, if he could help it.

"Oh! all right then, I'll go, Max, while you look out for my camera, like a good fellow. But see here, if you think I'll let anybody mistake me for the one who grabbed up this baby from the raft at the risk of his life, you've got another guess coming to you, that's right. I'm meaning to tell everybody that it was Max Hastings did it. Huh! any fellow could just keep hold of the end of a rope, and pull up like we did. That was the easiest part of it. You wait and see if you get out as slick as you think you will. They'll remember, and lay for you later on. If you will do these things, why, you've got to take your medicine, that's all."

So saying Steve hurried toward the shore, carrying the little child tenderly in his arms. Doubtless some one would be sure to recognize the small chap who had had such a narrow escape from a terrible fate; and if not just then, he would be well looked after until his folks turned up later on.

The wildest sort of reception was given Steve when he once got ashore. He could be seen trying to fend off the many hands that were outstretched to seize upon his digits, and give them a squeeze of approval, for deeds like this arouse the warmest sentiments in the human heart. In vain did Steve declare that it had been Max who had taken all the risks in the endeavor to save a precious little life; but the crowd would not keep back, and insisted that he let them do him honor. He had done his part in the rescue work at least, and was entitled to their congratulations, and they would not be denied.

Steve hastened to push his burden into the arms of the first woman who manifested the least desire to get hold of the child; and after that he pressed his way out of the crowd, heading once more for the imperiled bridge.

"Better come off there, now, Steven!" warned a gentleman who was standing near the approach to the structure; "there isn't one chance in a thousand that she'll hold out much longer, and it might be all your lives are worth to go down with the wreck when the time comes!"

But Steve was young, and filled with the spirit of adventure. Besides, after having been out there so long he had become partly used to the sickening tremor, and did not mind its warning as much as before.

"That's for Max to say, Mr. Harding," he called back. "If he thinks it's getting too dangerous for us, we'll sure come in right away. I've got to leave it with Max."

Two minutes later and he joined his chums, who were still near the middle of the bridge, again looking up the river anxiously.

"See another baby coming along?" demanded Steve, as he joined them.

"Not yet, I'm glad to say," replied Max, who was not so inflated over the grand success that had attended his first life saving effort that he wanted other opportunities to confront them immediately.

"L-l-looked like they came near p-p-pulling you to p-p-pieces, Steve," remarked Toby, with a grin.

"That's right," agreed Steve, frowning; "everybody tried to grab my hand at the same time, and me a telling them all the while I didn't have a thing to do with saving the child, only hauling on the rope. Say, I know now why you wouldn't go ashore, Max; you didn't want to be mobbed, did you? It's just terrible I'm telling you all. If I ever save anybody's life I'm going to take to the woods right away, till everybody forgets it."

"I saw Mr. Harding talking to you; what did he say?" asked Max, smiling a little to find that Steve was so modest.

"Oh! like a good many more of 'em he thinks we're taking too big chances staying right along out here, and that we ought to come ashore," Steve replied.

"He means it for our good, all right," ventured Bandy-legs, "and you know, fellers, he had a boy drowned year before last, so I reckon he's worried about us more than a little. What did you tell him, Steve?"

"That I'd leave it to Max here," came the reply.

"Which is putting a lot of responsibility on my poor shoulders," remarked that worthy, with a shrug.

"Well, you're our leader, and as long as we believe you know best we expect to follow out your ideas," Steve went on to say.

"That sounds pretty fine, Steve," observed Max; "but right now if I told you I thought we'd better go ashore you'd kick like a steer."

"Oh! well, you see there doesn't seem to be any very great danger as long as a big tree ain't swooping down to strike the bridge a crack; and besides, what if another baby happened to come sailing along on a raft, what'd we think of ourselves if we'd gone up on the bank, and couldn't even make a break to save it?"

Steve argued fairly well, and Max did not attempt to press the matter. To tell the truth he was tempted to linger to the very last in the hope of being instrumental in doing more good. If one child had been sent adrift in the flood, perhaps there might be others also in need of succor. And so Max, usually so cautious, allowed himself to be tempted to linger even when his better judgment warned him of the terrible risks they ran.

"Some of that crowd think we're sillies for staying out here, don't they, Steve?" Bandy-legs asked, after a little time had elapsed, without their sighting any more precious cargoes coming down on the flood.

"Yes, I heard a lot of 'em say things that way, because they've got a notion in their heads the bridge is agoin' out any old minute. But there's another lot that don't believe shucks. I heard one boy say there wasn't a bit of danger, and that we got all the credit of being mighty reckless and brave without taking any big risk."

"Bet you I can give a guess who that was," ventured Bandy-legs, instantly.

"Let's hear, then," Steve told him.

"It sounds like that braggin' Shack Beggs," was the guess Bandy-legs hazarded.

"Go up head, old scout," chuckled Steve; "because you hit it the first shot. Yes, that's who it was, Shack Beggs, and both the other bullies were along with him, watching everything we did out here, and looking like they'd be mighty well pleased if the old bridge did break loose and carry us all down river, hanging on like a parcel of half drowned rats."

"I wouldn't put it past them to help things along, if only they knew how they could start the bridge loose," Bandy-legs affirmed, positively, which showed what sort of an opinion he had for the trio of tough boys whom they had chased off, at the time they were robbing poor old Mr. McGirt, who kept the little candy shop that had been invaded by the rising waters.

"L-l-lucky for us they d-d-don't know h-h-how," said Toby, vigorously.

"It seems that when you get to talking about any one they're almost sure to appear," Max told them; "and look who's coming out on the bridge now."

"Why, it's Shack Beggs, sure it is!" declared Steve.

"Wonder what's he's up to?" muttered Bandy-legs. "We'd all better keep our peepers on that feller if he comes around. Why, I wouldn't put it past him to give one of us a sudden shove, and then laugh like he was crazy to see what a splash we made when we fell in. If I ketch him trying anything like that, mark my words Shack Beggs'll take a header into the river as quick as a flash. He'll find that two c'n play at that game!"

CHAPTER V

THE PRICE THEY PAID

"Look at him, would you?" ventured Bandy-legs, a minute later. "He acts like he was trying to see if the bridge was steady, the way he's trying to shake it. Bet you he feels that quivering, and it's giving him a bad case of cold feet already. They went and dared him to come out here, and Shack never would stand for a dare, you know. But he's sorry he came."

The other boy approached them. He was looking more serious than most people had ever seen him appear. Just as Bandy-legs said, no doubt he had been forced into testing the bridge by some dare on the part of his cronies, who had told him he didn't have the nerve to go Max and his crowd one better by walking all the way across the bridge, so as to be the last who could say he had done it.

While still keeping a sharp lookout up the river the four chums awaited the coming of Shack Beggs; and that the caution given by Bandy-legs had fallen on good ground where it took root, was proven by the way they moved back from the railing.

If the young desperado had any bold intention of trying to upset one of the three chums into the river, he would not find it so easy to carry out his reckless plan, for they were evidently on the alert, and ready to match cunning with cunning.

Shack shuffled forward slowly. He may have originally thought it would be the easiest thing in the world to walk across the bridge and back; but that was before he had set foot on the quivering planks, and experienced the full effect of that sickening vibration. Now he walked as though he might be stepping on eggs. Several times he even stopped, and looked around. Perhaps he simply wanted to know how far out from the shore he might be; or else he felt an almost irresistible yearning to hurry back to safety and tell his cronies they could try the trick for themselves, if they wanted.

Some sort of pride caused him to come on. Max and his friends were there, and Shack Beggs would sooner die than let them see he lacked the stamina they were so freely showing.

All the same he looked anything but happy as he drew closer. It was one thing to stand on a firm foundation ashore, and look out at the heaving flood, and another to find himself there surrounded by the waters, with but a slender thread connecting him with either bank, and all that furious flood trying its best to break this asunder.

"Better come back, Shack!" could be heard in a rasping voice from the shore, and Ossie Kemp was seen making a megaphone out of his two hands.

Shack would no doubt have liked to do this same thing; but he felt that it must look too much like cowardice in the eyes of Max, whom he hated so bitterly. Besides he had started out to show the people of Carson that these four chums did not monopolize all the courage in town; and it was really too late to turn back now.

So Shack came slowly on until he had reached the others.

Under ordinary conditions he would never have ventured to say a single word to any one of the four chums; or if he did, it would have probably been in the nature of an ugly growl, and some sarcastic comment on their personal appearance, with the sinister hope of provoking a dispute that might lead to a scuffle.

Things somehow seemed different now. Shack must have left most of his pugnacious disposition ashore; when his nerves were quivering with each sickening shake of the bridge he could not find it in him to assume his customary boastful look.

And seeing Max close Shack even ventured to speak decently to him, something he would never have dreamed of doing had the conditions been other than they were.

"The fellers they sez I dassent cross over tuh t'other end uh the bridge; an' I allowed it could be done easy like," he went on to say; "what d'ye think 'bout me adoin' the same? Is she safe enough?"

"We wouldn't be here if we didn't think so," Max told him; "and I guess there isn't any more danger on the other side than in the middle."

"T'anks!" Shack jerked out; and then as the bridge gave a little harder quiver than usual he looked frightened, and even clutched frenziedly at the railing.

Bandy-legs must have fancied that the other was reaching out to lay hands on him, for he immediately shouted:

"Keep back there! Don't you dare touch a finger to me, or I'll see that you go over the railing head-first! We're on to your sly tricks, Shack Beggs! You didn't come out here for nothing, I take it!"

Shack however had managed to overcome his sudden fear. He shot a black scowl in the direction of Bandy-legs, and then once more started to move along; but by now his timidity had over-mastered his valor, as was made manifest in the way he kept moving his hand along the railing, as though unwilling to try to stand alone.

Although they no longer had any reason to feel that the other meant them any ill turn, the four chums watched him curiously.

"I'd just like to be able to give the bridge a good shake," Bandy-legs declared, "to see him crumple up, and yell. Chances are it'd scare him out of a year's growth."

"Huh! better not try any fool play like that," suggested Steve; "because there's too much tremble to the old thing right now to suit me. If Max only said the word I'd be willing to skip out of this, that's right."

"S-s-s'pose we all did run for it," remarked Toby, who had been silent a long time; "wouldn't Shack come c-c-chasing after us like h-h-hot cakes, though?"

"We'll limit our stay to another five minutes, no more," Max told them. "I put it at that because I believe before then we'll be able to say whether that thing coming down the river is a raft with somebody aboard, or just a jumble of logs, and stuff set afloat by the high water."

Apparently none of the others had up to then noticed what Max referred to, and consequently there was a craning, of necks, and a straining of eyes, until Steve was fain to call out "rubber!" in his jocular way.

There was something in sight, far up the river. If they only had their field glass along with them it would be easy to tell the nature of the object; but lacking so useful an article they could only possess their souls in patience, and wait.

The seconds passed, and all the while the current of the river was bringing that object closer to them. Max found himself wishing it would hasten, for truth to tell he did not much like the way the bridge was trembling now. Instead of occasional vibrations it seemed to be a steady pull, as though the force of the flood had reached a point where it could not be much longer held back.

Some of those ashore were shouting to them again, as though their fears had broken out once more, and they wished the boys would not persist in taking such great chances, even though in a good cause.

A minute had gone.

"Looks like a raft to me," announced Bandy-legs, presently, and the others were inclined to agree with him that far.

"But is there any one aboard?" asked Max.

"I c'n see something there, but just what it might be I wouldn't like to say," the boy with the eagle eye announced.

Still they lingered, although those heavings were gradually growing a trifle more pronounced all the while. They must have shattered what little nerve Shack Beggs had remaining, for although he had not gone more than half way between the four chums and the further shore, he had turned around, and was now approaching them again. His face looked strangely ghastly, owing to his deadly fear; and the way in which Shack tried to force a grin upon it only made matters worse.

He had the appearance of one who was solemnly promising himself that if only he might be allowed to reach a haven of safety again he would never more be guilty of attempting such a silly act on account of a dare.

In fact, Shack was watching the chums eagerly every second of the time now. He depended on them to serve as his barometer. Should they make a sudden move toward the Carson side of the river he was in readiness to fairly fly along, in the hope of catching up with them.

Max turned his attention once more up the stream, and toward that approaching floating object. He wondered whether he was going to be called upon to once more make use of that friendly rope in rescuing some flood sufferer from peril.

After all Bandy-legs was not so sure about its being a raft. He began to hedge, and change his mind.

"Might be only a bunch of fence rails, and such stuff, that's got driven together in the flood, and is coming down on us in a heap," he announced. Max had about come to the same conclusion himself, though hesitating to announce his opinion while the others seemed to have an entirely different idea about the thing.

"But do you see that dark object on it move any?" he asked Bandy-legs.

"Well, now, seemed to me it did move just then," came the answer, that caused the boys to once more rivet their gaze on the approaching float, while their nerves began, to tingle with suspense.

A few seconds later and Toby declared that he too had seen the thing raise its head; though he hastily added:

"But it didn't act like a h-h-human b-b-being any that I could notice."

"What in the dickens can it be?" Steve was asking, and then he gave a sort of gasp, for the bridge had actually swayed in a way that caused. his heart to seemingly stand still.

"She's agoing to move out right away, I do believe, boys!" cried Bandy-legs, as he looked longingly toward the shore.

There was Shack Beggs almost half-way to the end of the bridge, and walking as fast as he could. From his manner it looked as though Shack would only too gladly have sprinted for the land, only that he hated to hear the jeering remarks which his cronies were sure to send at him for showing the white feather; so he compromised by walking ever so fast.

"Hadn't we better be going, Max?" asked Steve.

"That's the stuff!" muttered Bandy-legs.

"M-m-me too!" added Toby.

Max took one last look up the river. As he did so he saw that there was now a decided movement aboard the floating mass of stuff that was coming down toward the bridge.

Whatever it was that had been lying there now struggled to its feet.

"Oh! would you look at that?" exclaimed Steve.

"Must be a calf!" echoed Bandy-legs.

"I'd s-s-say a yeller dog!" Toby declared.

"Anyhow it's an animal and not a human being," said Max; "and things are getting too shaky for us to stay any longer out here, and take chances, just to try and save a dog or a calf or a goat. Let's put for the shore, boys!"

"And every fellow run for it too!" added Steve, as again they felt that terrible shudder pass through the wooden structure that had spanned the Evergreen Elver as far back as they could remember; and which somehow forcibly reminded Max of the spasm apt to run through the muscles of a stricken animal before giving up the ghost.

That was enough to start them with a rush. Once they gave way to the feeling that it was close on the breaking point for the bridge and what might be likened to a small-sized panic took possession of them all.

Shack Beggs somehow seemed to scent their coming. Perhaps he felt the vibrations increase, or else the shouts that both Steve and Bandy-legs gave utterance to reached his strained hearing.

At any rate Shack twisted his head, and looked back over his shoulder. If he had been anxious to reach the shore before, he was fairly wild now to accomplish that same object. They could see him take a spurt. He no longer deigned to walk, but ran as though in a race; as indeed all of them were, even though as yet they hardly comprehended the fact.

It might be possible that this was the worst thing the boys could have done, and that had they been contented to walk quietly toward land they might have spared the already badly racked bridge a new strain.

Max, looking back later on, came to this same conclusion; but, then he always declared that if one only knew how things were about to come out, he could alter his plans accordingly; in other words he quoted the old and familiar saying to the effect that "what wonders we could accomplish if our foresight were only as good as our hindsight."

The shaking of the structure by the scampering along of five boys must have been pretty much like the last straw added to the camel's pack.

"Faster, everybody!" Max shouted, as he heard a strange grinding noise that struck a cold chill to his very heart.

Bandy-legs was in front, and really setting the pace, and as everybody in Carson knew full well, he was the poorest pacemaker possible, on account of his exceedingly short and rather bent legs. This caused them to be held back more or less, though when it came down to actual figuring nothing they could have done would have altered the complexion of conditions.

The grinding noise turned into a frightful rending that sounded in their ears as though all sorts of superstructures might be separating. All the while there was a swaying of the timbers of the stricken bridge, a sickening sensation such as might be experienced when out at sea and caught in a cross current.

Max realized that it was useless for them to think of reaching the safety of the shore which was too far away; even Shack Beggs had been unable to accomplish the end he had in view, though he was still staggering on.

"Grab something, and keep holding on for all you're worth!"

That was about all Max could say, for hardly had the last word left his lips when there came a final jerk that threw them all down; and only for having caught hold of the railing one or more of the boys might have been tumbled into the river.

At the same time one end of the bridge broke away, the entire structure swung around so that it started to point down stream; then the strain caused the other end to also free itself from its moorings; after which the whole fabric fell over with a mighty splash, while the crowds ashore stared in horror at the spectacle, knowing as they did that the boys had been engulfed with the falling timbers.

CHAPTER VI

COMRADES IN DISTRESS

It was all a confused nightmare to the boys who went down with the bridge that the rising flood had finally carried away. They involuntarily gripped the railing tenaciously, because they had the last words of Max ringing in their ears; and no doubt it was this more than anything else that enabled them to come through the adventure with fair chances.

Max with his other hand had seized hold of Toby's arm, because they happened to be close together at the time. So it was that when he could catch his breath, after swallowing a gulp or two of muddy water, he called out:

"Are you all right, Toby?"

"Y-y-yep, s-s-seems so, Max!" he heard close to his ear in reply.

"What about the others? Steve, Bandy-legs, how is it with you?" continued Max, unable to see as yet, for his eyes were full of the spray that had dashed around them at the time the bridge carried them down.

Faint replies came to his ears, one from the left, and the other welling up in the opposite direction; but they cheered the heart of the leader greatly. It seemed almost like a miracle that all of them should have come through with so little damage. Looking back afterwards Max was of the opinion that much of this wonderful luck resulted from the fact that when the bridge swung around and allowed itself to be carried away it did not actually turn over.

They were being swept down-stream at a tremendous pace. Their strange craft rose and fell on the heaving flood with a sensation that might cause one to believe he had taken passage on the ocean itself, and was about to endure the discomforts of sea sickness.

Turning to look toward the shore Max realized for the first time how rapid was their passage; for when his eyes remained fixed on the water itself, which was making exactly the same speed as their craft, he seemed to be standing still.

"Max, oh! Max!" came in Steve's voice, a minute later.

"Hello! there, that you, Steve? Can't you make your way over here closer to us?" was the answer Max sent back; for now he could manage to glimpse the crouching figure from which the excited hail proceeded.

"Sure I can, easy as anything," Steve told him, and immediately proceeded to work along the railing, which fortunately remained above the water.

Bandy-legs had heard what was said, and from the other side he too came crawling along, moving like a crab backward, for he wished to keep his face toward the danger, since every dip of the whirling raft threatened to allow the waves to overwhelm him, as his position was not so secure as that of the others.

In this fashion, then, they gathered in a clump, gripping the railing with desperate zeal. Somehow or other the mere fact of getting together seemed to give each of the chums renewed courage.

"Ain't this a fierce deal, though?" Steve was saying, as drenched from head to foot he clung there, and looked at the swirling flood by which they found themselves surrounded, with the shore far away on either hand.

"B-b-beats anything I ever s-s-struck!" chattered Toby, whose teeth were apparently rattling like castanets, either from cold or excitement, possibly a little of both.

"We're in a tight hole, that's a fact," Max admitted, "but we ought to be thankful it's no worse than it is. One of us might have been swept loose, and drowned, or had a hard time getting around. We're all together, and it'll be queer if we can't figure out some way to get ashore, sooner or later."

"That's the ticket, Max; 'never give up the ship,' as Lawrence said long ago," was the way Steve backed the leader up.

"Huh!" grunted Bandy-legs, who had bumped his head, and because it felt sore he was not in the happiest mood possible; "that's just what we're wantin' to do, if you c'n call this turnin' twistin' raft a ship. Makes me dizzy the way she reels and cavorts; just like she might be trying one of them new fangled dance steps."

"Listen! what was that?" exclaimed Max, breaking in on Bandy-legs' complaint.

"What did you think you heard?" asked Steve, eagerly; "we're too far away from either shore right here to hope for anything, because you remember the banks of the Evergreen are low after passing our town, and the water's had a chance to spread itself. Whew! it must be half a mile across here, and then some."

"There it came again," said Max. "And seems to me it sounded like a half-drowned shout for help."

"What, away out here?" cried Steve; "who under the sun could be wanting us to give him a helping hand, d'ye think, Max?"

"I don't know, but at a time like this you can look for anything to happen. Perhaps there were other people carried away on the flood. Look around, and see if you can glimpse anything."

The water was not quite so riotous now, since it spread over a wider territory; and the boys had succeeded in getting their eyes clear; so that almost immediately Bandy-legs was heard to give a shout.

"I see him, fellers!" he announced, excitedly; "over yonder, and swimmin' to beat the band! He's tryin' to make the floating bridge we're on, but seems like the current keeps agrippin' him, and holdin' him back. Looks like he's mighty near played out in the bargain."

"Why, however could he have got there, and who is he, d'ye reckon, Max?" Steve inquired, turning as usual to the leader when a knotty problem was to be solved.

"I think I know," replied Max, without hesitation; "you seem to have forgotten that we weren't alone on the bridge when it fell."

"Oh! shucks! yes, you mean that Shack Beggs!" Bandy-legs suggested, and there was a vein of disappointment and indifference in his voice that Max did not like.

True, that same Shack Beggs had been one of the most aggressive of their foes in Carson. From away back he in company with a few other choice spirits of like mean disposition had never let an opportunity for annoying the chums pass. On numerous occasions he had planned miserable schemes whereby Max, or some of his best friends, would be seriously annoyed.

All the same that could be no excuse for their turning a deaf ear to the wild appeal for help which the wretched Shack was now sending forth. He was human like themselves, though built on different lines; and they could never hold their own respect if they refused to hold out a helping hand to an enemy in dire distress.

"We've just got to try to get Shack up here with us, boys, if the chance comes our way," said Max, firmly.

"S'pose we have," muttered Bandy-legs, moodily; and his manner was as much as to say that in his opinion the young scoundrel struggling there in the water was only getting something he richly deserved; and that if it rested with him he would feel inclined to let Shack stay there until the extreme limit.

"But how can we do anything for him, Max?" asked Steve, who was not so bitter as Bandy-legs, and already began to feel a little compassion toward the wretched boy struggling so desperately in the agitated water, and nearly exhausted by his efforts.

"There's a small chance," said Max, who had been looking more closely than any of his chums. "You see this piece of the broken bridge keeps on turning around in the water all the while. Now we've got the west shore on our right hand, and pretty soon we'll have the east side that way. Well, perhaps we'll swing around next time far enough for us to stretch out and give Shack a helping hand."

"I believe you're right, Max," admitted Steve; "yes, she's swinging right along, and if he's wise he'll work in this way as much as he can. But, Max, if we do pass him by without being able to reach him, it's going to be hard on Shack, because he looks like he's nearly all in, and won't be on top when we come around again."

"Then we've just got to reach him, you see!" returned Max, with that glow in his eyes the others knew so well, for it generally meant success to follow.

The fragment of the broken bridge continued to move around as the swirl of the waters kept turning it. Max was watching eagerly, and making his calculations with as much earnestness as though it were one of his chums in peril instead of their most bitter enemy.

He believed there was a good chance for him to reach Shack, if he could manage in some way to stretch out from the end of the railing just beyond where Toby clung. And acting on this inspiration he hastily clambered past the other.

"What's doing, Max?" demanded Toby, immediately.

"If I can reach him at all it's got to be from the end of the raft here, the further point, don't you see?" Max replied, still pushing along, with Toby close at his heels, ready now to assist to the best of his ability.

So Max, on reaching the extreme tip of the uneasy raft, climbed out as far as he could go, and called back to Toby to grip him by the legs so that he might have both hands free to work with when the critical moment arrived.

It could not be long delayed, for as they swung slowly in the grip of the swirling current he could see the swimming Shack's head close by. Once the almost exhausted boy disappeared, and Max felt his heart give a great throb as he thought it was the very last he would ever see of Shack; but almost immediately afterwards the head came in sight again, for Shack was a stout fellow, and desperation had nerved him to accomplish wonders.

Presently Max gritted his teeth together for the effort he meant to put forth, and upon which so much depended.

"Swim this way as hard as you can, Shack!" he had shouted again and again, and the boy in the river was evidently bent on doing what he was told, though hardly able to sustain himself on account of complete exhaustion, added to a severe case of fright.

Then the crisis came. Max had figured nicely, and knew to a fraction of a second just when he must make his clutch for the swimmer. Shack saw what was coming, and as though ready to give up and sink if this effort to save him failed, he threw out one of his hands despairingly toward Max.

As he managed to clutch the swimmer's wrist Max braced himself, and gradually drew Shack toward the woodwork of the floating bridge, an inch as it were at a time, but constantly coming.

Presently he had him close enough for Steve, who with Bandy-legs was near by, to get a frenzied grip on the other arm of the exhausted boy; and then together they managed to help him aboard.

It was necessary that they change their position quickly, since their combined weight at one end of the wreckage of the bridge was causing it to sink in an ominous way.

"Move along there, Bandy-legs and Steve!" called Max; "or we'll be under water!"

Fortunately the other boys realized what was meant, and they hurried away, constantly clinging to the friendly railing which had proven so valuable all the while, in keeping them from being washed overboard.

Max helped Shack crawl along, for the boy was panting for breath, and almost choked with the vast quantities of water he had swallowed.

In this way they presently reached their old positions about the middle of the floating timbers. It was a wild picture that confronted them as they now took the time to look around them. The river was narrowing somewhat again and of course the current became considerably swifter on this account, so that the bridge raft rocked violently back and forth, sometimes even threatening them with a fresh disaster in the shape of a jam, and consequent overturn.

"My stars! what's the answer going to be to this thing?" Steve called out, after one of these exciting experiences, during which it was with considerable difficulty that the whole of them maintained their hold.

Max had seen to it that the tired Shack was fastened to the rail with a strap he chanced to have in his pocket at the time; only for that possibly the other might have lost his weakened grip, and been carried off.

"Oh! don't think of giving up yet, Steve," Max sang out cheerily; "the further we get downstream the more chances there are that we'll either be rescued by men in boats, or else find a way ourselves to get ashore. We've got so much to be thankful for that it seems as if we'd soon hit on a way out. Keep watching, and if some eddy in the current happens to throw us on a bar close to the shore, we'll hustle to reach land the best we know how, no matter where it is, or how far from home."

"T-t-that's what I s-s-say," stammered Toby; "all I w-w-want is to feel the g-g-good old g-g-ground under my f-f-feet again. I never thought it could be so n-nice as it seems right now."

"You never miss the water till the well runs dry!" chanted Bandy-legs, now getting over his fit of depression, and beginning to pluck up new courage and spirits.

"We are whooping it up at a mile a minute clip, ain't we, Max?" Steve asked, a short time later.

"Well, I'd hardly like to say that, Steve," answered the other; "but we're certainly making pretty swift time, twenty miles an hour, perhaps nearer thirty, I'd say. And that's going some, considering that we haven't any motor to push us along."

"And didn't they tell me it was about twenty miles down the valley that Asa French lived?" Steve went on to say, showing that even in the dreadful grip of the flood he had remembered that Bessie French was somewhere down below, and possibly also exposed to the perils that threatened all who lived along the banks of the furious Evergreen River.

Max too had given more than a few thoughts to this fact during the earlier part of that eventful day.

"The way we're going," he told Steve, "we ought to be down there before a great while; and let's hope we'll strike luck, and get a chance to go ashore."

"And also find the girls all right," added Steve, who had apparently quite forgotten how Bessie had recently cut him cruelly, while suffering from an unfortunate misunderstanding.

"But what ails Toby there; he seems to be excited over something?" Max went on to exclaim; for Toby was bending forward, and showed plain evidences of growing interest.

"Hey! fellers!" he now burst out with, "just looky there, will you? We're in for a f-f-fresh lot of t-t-trouble seems like. W-w-watch him p-p-pop up again, would you? Whew! but he's a b-b-bouncer, too, biggest I ever saw in my born days, and must be twenty feet long. Max, it's a s-s-sure enough s-s-sea serpent, ain't it, now?"

CHAPTER VII

THE SUBMERGED FARM-HOUSE

"Gee whiz! where is it, Toby?" cried Steve. "And none of us got a gun along, worse luck. Hey, show me the sea serpent, and p'raps my camera ain't so wet but what I might crack off a picture of the same; because nobody's ever going to believe you when you tell that yarn. Show me, Toby!"

Toby was only too willing to comply. He had always had a decided weakness for collecting all sorts of wild animals, and that might explain why he displayed such extraordinary excitement now.

"There, right over past the end of the r-r-raft, where it s-s-sticks up like a c-c-church spire!" he stuttered, pointing as he spoke. "Now watch everybody, when he pokes his old h-h-head up again. There, don't you s-s-see? And s-s-say, he seems to be s-s-swimmin' this way, don't he?"

Steve broke out into a yell.

"Why, bless your old timid soul, Toby, that isn't any snake at all, only one of those big wild-grape vines, like enough, that's ketched on to that floating tree trunk close by. She's all twisted and turned, and I reckon a fellow as crazy over wild animals and things, like you are, might be excused for thinkin' it was a regular sea serpent."

Bandy-legs too was showing amusement.

"Guess that's the way nearly all sea serpents are discovered," he remarked, trying to make it appear as though he had not been almost as excited as Toby, when the other burst out so suddenly with his announcement.

"Well, we haven't lost any snakes," commented Max, "and so we won't try to rescue that floating vine. We've had our turn at saving menageries, seems to me, enough for one season anyway."

What Max referred to was a series of remarkable adventures that came to the four chums at a time when a storm blew down the tents belonging to a circus about to exhibit in Carson, and liberating many of the animals connected with the menagerie; but full particulars of this thrilling experience have already been given in the volume preceding this, so that further explanation would seem to be unnecessary here.

Toby did not make any reply. He rubbed his eyes pretty hard, as though wondering how they could have deceived him so strangely. But then a fellow who was devoting so much of his thoughts to the mania for strange pets in the shape of wild animals might be expected to see things in a different light from his chums, who were not addicted to that weakness.

"For one," said Bandy-legs, "I'm real glad it wasn't a snake, because they always give me the creeps, you remember, I hate 'em so. Just think what a fine pickle we'd be in now if a monster anaconda or a big boa constrictor or python, broke loose from a show, should climb up on our bridge boat, and start to chasin' us all overboard. Things look bad enough as they are without our takin' on a bunch of new trouble. So, Toby, please don't glimpse anything else, and give us fits, will you?"

Steve seemed to be intently watching the shore, especially whenever the revolving timbers brought them in a line with the western bank, because that was more familiar to the boys than the other, since Carson lay on that side of the river toward the setting sun.

"I'm trying to make out where we are, Max," he explained, upon seeing that the other was observing him curiously.

Bandy-legs uttered a loud and significant grunt.

"Say, Steve," he remarked with a touch of satire in his voice, "I can tell you that much, if you're all mixed up. We're squattin' on the remains of our bloomin' bridge, which used to cross the river in front of Carson; yes-siree, and we seem to be takin' an unexpected voyage downstream, without a port in sight. 'Water, water everywhere, and not a drop to drink,' as the ship-wrecked sailor used to sing; only we could manage with this muddy stuff if we had to, because it ain't salty, you know."

"How far have we come, Max?" Steve continued, anxious to know, and pretending to pay no attention to Bandy-legs' humorous remarks.

"I'm trying to figure it out myself, Steve," admitted the other, who had also been studying the shore line, though everything was so changed during the high water that it was difficult to recognize land marks that had previously been quite familiar to him; "and the best I can make out is that we must be somewhere near Dixon's Point, where the river makes that first sharp curve."

"And, Max, that's about fifteen miles below Carson, isn't it?" Steve added, as he twisted his head the better to look down-stream again.

"Something like fifteen or sixteen, Steve."

"And if Asa French's place is twenty, we ought to strike in there right soon, hadn't we, Max?"

"Before ten minutes more, like as not," Max told him.

Steve drew in a long breath. He was undoubtedly wondering what the immediate future had in store for them, and whether some strange fortune might not bring him in close touch with Bessie. He doubtless had been picturing this girl friend of his in all sorts of thrilling situations, owing to the rapidly rising river, and always with some one that looked suspiciously like Steve Dowdy rushing valiantly to the relief of the helpless ones.

Steve had once tried to play the hero part, and stopped what he believed was a runaway horse, with Bessie in the vehicle, only to have her scornfully tell him to mind his own business after that, since he had spoiled her plans for proving that their old family nag still had considerable speed left in him.

Steve had never forgotten the scorn and sarcasm that marked the girl's face and voice when she said that to him. It had come back to his mind many times since that occasion; and he had kept aloof from all social events ever since, because he did not mean to be snubbed again. And even now, when he was picturing Bessie in real trouble, he kept telling himself that he meant to make sure she was surely in danger of drowning, or something like that, before he ventured to try and succor her. "Because," Steve told himself, "once bit, twice shy; and not if I know it will I ever give any girl the chance again to say I'm trying to show off."

All the same his eyes seldom roved in any other quarter now but down-stream, which was mute evidence that Steve was thinking about other peoples' troubles besides his own.

"We couldn't do anything to help move this old raft closer to shore, could we, Max?" Bandy-legs was suggesting.

"Hardly, though I'd like to first-rate," he was told; "but it's too cumbersome for us to move it, even if we pulled off some boards to use as paddles. So it looks as if we'd have to trust to luck to take us in the right quarter for making our escape."

"Well, we can be ready, and if the chance comes, make the plunge," Bandy-legs continued, "We're all so wringing wet as it is that if we had to jump in and swim a piece it wouldn't hurt any. Just remember that I'm ready if the rest of you are. I'm not caring any too much for this sort of a boat. It keeps on turning around too many times, like a tub in a tub race, and you never know what minute you're going to be dumped out, if it takes a notion to kick up its heels and dive."

"Don't look a g-g-gift horse in the m-m-mouth, Bandy-legs!" advised Toby.

Steve was manifesting more and more restlessness.

"Max, you've been down this far before, I reckon, even if most all our camping trips were to the north and west of Carson?" he asked, turning to the leader.

"Yes, several times, to tell you the truth," admitted Max; "but with the flood on, things look so different ashore that it's pretty hard to tell where you are. Why do you ask me that, Steve?"

"Do you remember whether there's a bend about a mile or so above the French farm house?" continued Steve.

After reflecting for several seconds Max gave his answer.

"Yes, you're right, there is; and I should say it must lie about a mile or so this side of the place."

"I was trying to figure it all out," Steve told him, "and it's this way it looks like to me. The current will sweep us across the river when we swing around that same bend, won't it?"

"Pretty far, for a fact, Steve, because it's apt to run the same way even if the river is far out of its regular channel now."

"Well, don't you see that's going to bring us pretty close to where the French house used to lie?" Steve remarked, inquiringly.

"Yes, it might, just as you say," Max replied; "but why do you speak of it in that way — used to lie?"

"Because," said Steve, moodily, "I'm scared to think what might have happened to that same house by now, and wondering if it's been swept clean away; though it was a strongly built place, and ought to stand a heap of pounding before it went down."

"But even if it isn't in sight, Steve, that doesn't mean the girls have been carried away on the flood, or else drowned. Of course Asa French would be warned long enough ahead to hitch up his horses, and pull-out for higher ground with everybody in his family. They're all right, the chances are ten to one that way."

Max said this for a purpose. He saw that Steve was feeling dreadfully about it, and knew the discovery would be doubly hard should they come upon the place where the French farm house had stood, to find it missing; and so he wanted to prepare the other chum against a shock.

"It's kind of you to say that, Max," Steve faltered, swallowing a lump that seemed to be choking him; "and I'm going to try and believe what you tell me. We ought to know the worst soon, now, because we're just above that bend, and already I can see how the current sets in as swift as anything toward the other shore."

All of them fell silent after that. They were watching the way the floating timbers of the lost bridge were being steadily swept toward the west shore, or rather where that bank had once been, because a great sea of water now covered the fertile farmland for a distance of a mile or so, to where the hills began.

Shack Beggs had recovered his usual ability to look after himself, and while he did not say anything, there was a look on his face that set Max to thinking, as he thrust the strap into the hand of his rescuer, as though he would have no further need of it, and disliked appearing weaker than the rest in that he had to be fastened to the railing.

Shack had just passed through a thrilling experience that was fated to make a decided impression on his mind. He had hated these boys for years, and done all he could to make life miserable for them; it remained to be seen whether there would be any material change in his habits after this, or if he would forget his obligations to Max Hastings, and go right along as before.

Max would have pondered this matter, for it must have presented exceedingly interesting features to a fellow like him; but there was really no time for considering such things now. They would have all they could do to find a way to gain the shore, and cheat the flood of its prey. Max could not forget that some twenty miles below where they were now the river plunged over a high dam; and even in time of flood this might prove to be their Waterloo, if they were prevented from getting on land before the broken bridge timbers reached that obstruction.

"Now, look, everybody, because we're turning the bend!" Steve called out, in his great excitement hardly knowing what he was saying.

Eagerly they strained their eyes. The strange craft swung around the bend, and continued to keep edging toward the west side of the river. A broad expanse of turgid water met their eyes, broken here and there with a few objects such as treetops.

Once there had been numerous barns and out-buildings connected with the French farm, but everything had apparently been swept clean away saving the house itself, and that still stood, although the flood was even then three quarters of the way up to the gutters of the roof, and must be exerting a tremendous pressure that could not much longer be baffled.

"Oh! it's still standing, Max!" shouted Steve, hoarsely; "who'd ever think it could have held out so long? I tell you that's a bully old house, and built like a regular Gibraltar. But, Max, don't you glimpse something up there clinging to the roof? Somehow I don't seem able to see as clear as I might; I don't know what's the matter with me."

But Max knew that Steve was blinking as fast as he could, to dry the tears that had come unbidden into his eyes under the excess of his emotions.

"I honestly believe it's the girls!" he exclaimed, startled himself at making such a thrilling discovery.

Steve gave a cry of dismay.

"Whatever can they be doing up there; and where's Bessie's Uncle Asa, that he's left them all alone in the storm? Oh! Max, we've just got to work over to the house and help them. Do you think we're heading that way fast enough? Ain't there any way we could help the old raft to hurry up, and strike the house so we could climb up there? Well, if the worst comes I'm meaning to swim for it, current or no current."

"Wait and see!" cautioned Max; "I'm still thinking we'll swing far enough around to strike against the upper side of the house. I only hope the blow doesn't finish things, and topple the submerged building over."

This gave Steve something new to worry over. He started to shouting, and waving his hat vigorously, and received answering signals from those who were perched on the sloping roof of the farmhouse.

Doubtless the ones in peril may have been praying for rescuers to heave in sight, but certainly it could never have entered into their heads to conjure up such a strange way for assistance to come to them, in the shape of a raft composed of the timbers of the wrecked Carson bridge.

But so great had been their terror, when surrounded by those wild and rising waters, that no doubt they gladly welcomed the possibility of help in any shape. Besides, the coming of those four husky and resourceful lads was a thing not to be despised. Though they may not have owned a motorboat, or even a skiff, they had sturdy arms and active brains, and would surely find some way to serve those who just then seemed to be in great need of assistance.

CHAPTER VIII

REFUGEES OF THE ROOF

"Hi! here's more trouble!" cried Bandy-legs, while they were approaching the inundated farmhouse, borne on the sweeping current of the flood.

"What's the matter now?" called Steve, so anxious about the safety of those who clung to the sloping roof of the doomed building that he would not even turn his head all the way around, but shot the words back over his shoulder.

"Why, the blooming old wreck's going all to pieces, so that we'll each have to pick out a timber, and straddle mighty soon, if it keeps on this way!" Bandy-legs informed him.

This caused Max to take a little survey in order to satisfy himself that what the other said was true. What he discovered did not bring much assurance of comfort. Just as the sharp-eyed chum had declared, the remnant of the broken bridge was being by degrees torn apart by the violence of its fall and the subsequent action of conflicting currents of water.

It materially changed his plans, formed on the spur of the moment, when they had discovered the victims of the flood on the roof of the farmhouse. Instead of taking them off, as he had at first intended, it now began to look as though he and his comrades would be compelled to seek refuge alongside the girls.

This was not a pleasant thought, for Max could see that the building was very near the collapsing point as it was, and might topple over at any minute.

Max was, however, a boy who would accept what fortune offered, and do the best he could with it. Once on the roof, they could turn their attention to some other method of escape; at any rate they had no choice in the matter.

"We've got to climb up where they are, that's plain," he observed; "and if this stuff strikes the end of the house we'll be lucky enough."

"Then do we have to let it go, and be marooned up there?" asked Bandy-legs, in a forlorn tone.

"Looks that way," Steve went on to say, and somehow he did not seem to share the gloom that had gripped Bandy-legs, possibly because it began to look as though the glorious chance had come at last to show the girls he could do his duty without any boasting, and never meant to pose as a great hero.

"But why can't we hold on to some of these timbers, and make a jolly old raft?" Bandy-legs continued eagerly.

"Hurrah! that's the t-t-ticket!" Toby was heard to remark; "I never yet read about a R-r-robinson C-c-crusoe but what he made him a r-r-raft!"

"It might be a good idea, boys," admitted Max, "but I'm afraid you'll find it more than you can manage. Then besides, even if you did get some of the timbers to stick there, how could you fasten them together so as to make that raft? Show me your ropes and I'll join in with you mighty quick. But it isn't going to be the easiest thing going to climb up that wobbly roof; and we'll all be glad to find ourselves perching up on that ridge-pole with the girls, I think."

That dampened the enthusiasm and ardor of Bandy-legs considerably. Like the rest of them he realized that what Max said was about true, and that they could not expect to pay much attention to the parting timbers, once they reached the house. It would be all they could do to get up on the roof.

"Are we going to hit up against it, Max?" asked Steve, struggling between hope and fear, as they rapidly bore down toward the partly submerged farm building.

"Yes, there's no doubt about that," came the quick reply; "and come to think of it, we can get up where they are better by working our way around to that lower end to the right. Every fellow look out for himself when the time comes."

"Give us the word, Max?" Steve asked.

"All right, when you hear me shout 'now,' make your jump, and be sure you've picked out the right place beforehand, or you may drop back again."

Max could say no more, because they were so close to the little island in the midst of the raging flood that he had to conserve his breath in order to make a successful leap himself.

On the roof crouched the two girls, Bessie French and Mazie Dunkirk, together with a little lame cousin of the former, a girl of about eight. All of them were greatly interested in the coming of the boys, and stared eagerly at the remarkable craft that was bearing them on the surface of the flood. Perhaps they may have already jumped to the conclusion that the whole town of Carson had been inundated and swept away, and that these five lads might be the sole remaining survivors. That thought would in part account for their white faces; though of course their own perilous situation was enough to give them pale cheeks.

Max was on the alert. Just as the timbers came alongside the lower edge of the roof he shot out that one energetic word:

"Now!"

Immediately every fellow was in motion, and as they had selected their landing places beforehand, they fortunately did not interfere with each other's movements. Such a remarkable scrambling as followed; if you have ever watched a cat that has made too risky a jump, barely get her claws fastened on a limb, and then strain to clamber up, you can imagine something of the efforts of Toby and Bandy-legs in particular, as they did not seem to be quite as fortunate as the others.

But none of them dropped back into the river, and that was worth noticing. The girls continued to utter various exclamations of alarm and excitement as they watched their supposed-to-be rescuers trying to join them on the roof. Bessie even clapped her hands when Bandy-legs after a series of contortions that would have done credit to a professional athlete, managed to crawl over the edge, assisted by a hand given him, not from Max, nor yet Steve, but the despised Shack Beggs, who seemed to have had no difficulty whatever in making the landing, for he was a muscular fellow, and as wiry as a cat.

So they climbed up the slope of the submerged farm house, and joined those who were already perched along the ridgepole, like so many birds awaiting the time for flight.

Bandy-legs watched the timbers bumping against the side of the house until they parted company, and floated swiftly away in smaller sections. He felt like waving a sad farewell after the strange craft that had borne them all the way down the valley; never would he forget how it looked, passing away in pieces, as though its mission had been completed after allowing them to reach the farm-house.

There had been three refugees of the flood on the roof before; now their number had increased to eight. But whether the coming of the boys added anything to the hopefulness of the situation remained to be proved.

At least it seemed to have cheered up both girls considerably. Mazie welcomed the coming of Max when he climbed to a place beside her, with a look that was intended to be sunny, but bordered on the pitiful. Truth to tell the poor girl had just passed through the most terrible experience of her young life, having had responsibility crowded upon her in the absence of older heads.

"Oh! I am so glad you have come to help us, Max!" she told him, after they had shaken hands like good friends, which they always had been.

Max tried to laugh at that; he thought there was altogether too much gloom in the gathering, and it would be better for all hands to discover some sort of rift in the clouds.

"A queer old way of coming to help you, I should say, Mazie," he told her. "What you saw floating off after it carried us here was all that is left of the Carson bridge, which was carried away by the flood an hour or so ago."

"Oh! were there many people on it when it fell?" asked Bessie French, her eyes filled with suspense; she had pretended not to pay any attention to Steve, who had deliberately found a place beside her, and was sitting there as though he had a perfect right, and that nothing disagreeable had ever come up between them; but in spite of her seeming indifference she was watching him out of the tail of her eye all the same, just as a girl will.

"I'm glad to say that we were the only ones who went down with the bridge," Max hastened to tell her, knowing that she had loved ones in Carson, about whose safety she must naturally feel anxious.

"And all of you managed to cling to the timbers of the bridge?" questioned Mazie, looking with open admiration, first at Max, and then those with him, until a puzzled frown came on her pretty face, for she had finally noticed Shack Beggs, and could not understand how a boy of his bad reputation chanced to be in the company of Max and his chums.

"Yes, it wasn't so hard, after we got settled in the water," Max explained. "We had the railing to help us out. And a little later we managed to help Shack in out of the wet, for he was on the bridge at the same time, being thrown into the water when it collapsed."

"What a strange thing that you should be carried right down to where we were in such dreadful need of help; and on such a remarkable boat, too," Mazie went on to say, with a tinge of color in her cheeks now, which spoke volumes for the confidence she felt in the ability of this particular boy to discover some means for bringing about their eventual rescue.

"Well, it does seem so," Max replied; "and the funny thing about it was that Steve here, just a short time before the bridge fell, was saying he would give anything he had in the wide world for the loan of a motorboat, so he could run down here and see if you girls needed help."

That was cleverly meant for Bessie's ears; trust Max to put in a good word for his chum, because he knew how matters stood, and that Bessie was treating poor Steve rather shabbily. The girl flushed, and then slowly turning her face until her eyes, now dim with unshed tears, met the eager ones of the boy at her side, she leaned her head forward and said in a low voice:

"I'm going to ask you to forget all that's happened between us, Steve; and let's start over being friends. I'll never laugh at you again when you're honestly trying to do something for me. I was a little fool that time; but it'll never happen again, Steve. You'll forgive me, won't you?"

Of course, when Steve felt that little hand in his, he laughed good-naturedly, and was heard to say in return:

"Never bother myself thinking about it again, Bessie; give you my word on it. When I got home that time, and saw myself in a glass, I made up my mind that I looked like a scarecrow, and that any girl would be ashamed to have such a tramp stop her horse, whether he was running away or not. And we're all mighty glad we were on the old bridge when she took that drop, because it's been kind enough to carry us to you girls down here."

All this may have been very interesting, but Max knew they had no business to be wasting time in talking when confronted by a renewal of perils. The farm-house had stood out against the pressure of the flood in a way that was wonderful; but it must have a limit to its endurance, which he did not doubt had been nearly reached.

What would happen to them if it should suddenly collapse was not a pleasant subject for thought; and yet there could be no dodging the responsibility.

At the same time he was curious to know how it happened that the two girls and the little crippled cousin of Bessie came to be there alone; when it might have been expected that Asa French, or his farm hand, would be along, capable of rendering more or less assistance.

"How do you come to be here alone, you girls?" he hastened to ask of Mazie.

"It was just through a succession of accidents," the girl replied. "You see, Mr. French and his wife received a message from Alderson yesterday calling them over in great haste to visit an old aunt who was sinking, and from whom they expected to inherit quite a large sum of money. They disliked leaving us here, but we insisted on it; and besides the faithful old man who had been with them for just ages, Peter Rankin, promised to guard us well. They were to come back this morning, but I suppose the floods kept them from setting out, as the roads must all be under water between here and Alderson."

"And you've had a night of terror, with the water creeping up all the while," observed Max; "but what became of Peter Rankin; I hope he wasn't drowned?"

"We don't know," replied Mazie, with a tremor in her voice. "Three hours ago he left us, saying that the only hope was for him to try and swim to the shore, so as to get a boat of some kind, and come to our rescue before the house was carried away. We saw the brave old man disappear far down the river, and we've been hoping and praying ever since that at least he managed to get ashore. Then we discovered all that timber coming around the bend above, with people aboard, and none of us could even guess what it meant."

"Well," said Max, "we're here, all right, and the next thing to do is to find some way of getting to the bank below."

"Then you're afraid the house will go before long?" Mazie asked him; "and that's what I've been thinking would happen every time that queer tremble seemed to pass through it. We shrieked right out the first time, but I suppose we've become partly used to it by now. But, Max, what can we do?"

"I suppose there's nothing inside that could be used in place of a boat?" he asked, thoughtfully.

"Nothing but the furniture that is floating around the rooms; though some of that has been washed out, and disappeared," Mazie told him.

"Then we'll have to look around and see what can be done to make a raft. There are five of us boys, all stout enough to do our share of the work. We might manage to get some doors off their hinges, and fasten them together some way or other, if Bessie could only tell us where a clothes line was to be found."

Max tried to speak quietly, as though there was no need of being alarmed; but after experiencing one of those tremors Mazie mentioned, he realized that the foundations of the farm-house were being rapidly undermined by the action of the swift running water, so that it was in danger of being carried away at any minute.

No one could say just what would happen when this catastrophe came to pass; the house might simply float down-stream, partly submerged; or it was liable to "turn turtle," and become a mere wreck, falling to pieces under the attacks of the waters.

And if they were still clinging to that sloping roof when this occurred they would find themselves cast into the flood, half a mile away from shore, and at the mercy of the elements.

Yes, there was sore need of doing something, by means of which they might better their condition; and Max Hastings was not the one to waste precious minutes dallying when action was the only thing that could save them.

CHAPTER IX

PREPARING FOR THE WORST

Upon making further inquiries Max learned that there was a trap in the roof, through which the girls had crept, with many fears and misgivings, when the encroaching water within warned them that it was no longer safe to stay there.

Looking through this he could see that the place was fully inundated. Chairs and table were floating, and even the ladder which the girls had used was partly washed out of a window.

"Nothing much doing down there for us," Max informed Bandy-legs, who had crept over to the hole in the roof along with him, in order to satisfy his curiosity.

He had heard Max ask questions of the girls, and was deeply interested in learning what the next step might chance to be. Bandy-legs was still secretly mourning the fact that they had been compelled to let all that wreckage of the bridge get away from them. It had served them so splendidly up to that time, and still thinking of the Crusoe affair, he could not help believing that it had been a big mistake not to have at least made some effort to hold on to what they could.

"And to think," said Bandy-legs, sadly, "I've got the best sort of a life preserver at home you ever saw; but what good is it to me now?"

"But you can swim, all right," remarked Max.

"Oh! I wasn't thinking about myself that time, but what a fine thing it'd be to strap it around one of the girls right now. I say, Max, whatever are we agoin' to do with the three, if the old coop does take a notion to cut loose?"

"Not so loud, Bandy-legs," warned Max, with a little hiss, and a crooked finger. "We don't want them to know how tough things really are. If the worst does come we'll have to do what we can to keep them afloat; but I'm still hoping we may get some doors out that would be better than nothing, to hold on to in the water."

"I heard Bessie tell you that there was a clothesline hanging to a hook inside there, before the water came, and that it might be there yet if not washed away," Bandy-legs went on to remark.

"Yes, it wasn't very encouraging," Max informed him; "but I'm going inside and see if I can find it."

"You'll want help with the doors, too, of course, Max?"

"And I know where to look for it when you're around, Bandy-legs, because you're one of the most accommodating fellows on earth," the other told him.

"I'm about as wet as can be, so it doesn't matter a whiff what happens to me from now on," remarked the other boy; "but if we have to do more or less swimmin' while we're in there, Max, hadn't we better take our shoes off? I never could do good work with the same on."

"That's what I'm meaning to do, Bandy-legs; and there's no need of our waiting around any longer, so here goes."

Saying which Max proceeded to remove his wet shoes and socks, rolling his trouser legs up half way to his knees.

"What's all this mean?" asked Steve, crawling over to where the other two had gone; "looks like you had a scheme in mind."

He was quickly told what Max purposed doing.

"It doesn't seem like it'd amount to a great deal," he suggested.

"Huh! can you knock your coco and think up anything better, then; we'd sure be delighted to hear it," Bandy-legs told him; but Steve was not very fertile when it came to planning things, and he shook his head sadly.

"Wish I could, that's right," he said; "I'd give a heap right now to be able to snap my fingers, and have a nice little, power-boat happen along, so I could invite everybody to take a cruise with me. But there's no such good luck, And, Max, when you duck inside here, count on me to be along with you to do whatever I can."

"I knew you'd say that, Steve," observed the other, as though pleased to hear such a hearty response to his mute appeal.

Then came the other two, wondering what the plan of campaign might be; for even Shack Beggs, finding himself so strangely thrown in with these boys whom in the past he had hated and scorned; was already as deeply interested in the outcome as any of the chums might be; and Bandy-legs no longer frowned at his proximity, for he could not forget how it was Shack's strong hand that had helped him make a landing on the sloping roof just a short time before.

They dropped inside the house, and immediately found themselves up to their necks in water. Max took his bearings, and was pleased to discover that the coil of clothes line still hung from the hook, the water not having disengaged it as yet. Somehow the small success of finding this seemed to give him renewed courage.

"Things are beginning to come our way, fellows!" he called out, as he held the coil up above his head triumphantly.

"Hurray!" gurgled Toby, for it happened that just then he made a slip, and had a mouthful of muddy water come aboard, almost choking him.

"And here's this door swung loose," called out Steve, who had been working for several minutes, with the aid of Shack, to get the article in question off its hinges.

"Wait till I tie one end of the line to it," Max told them, "and then we can push it out and let it float behind the house. There isn't so much strength to the current there, on account of the eddies."

This was speedily done, and the floating door anchored, thanks to the friendly offices of the clothes line.

"That might do to hold up one of the girls," remarked Bandy-legs.

"It will," put in Steve, quickly; "and pretty fairly at that, because Bessie isn't so very heavy, you know."

Well, no one blamed Steve for pre-empting the first raft for the use of Bessie, because he had been chiefly instrumental in securing it.

"We ought to have two more, anyway," suggested Bandy-legs.

"And we'll get 'em, never fear," Steve assured him; "because there's just that many in sight. Here, Shack, give me another lift, will you? There isn't a fellow along got the strength in his arms you have, and that's the truth."

Shack Beggs looked pleased. It must have been a novel sensation for him to hear his praises sung by one of the chums of Max Hastings. They had called down anything but blessings on his head for many moons, yes, years, on account of the way he had annoyed them.

It was no easy task removing those doors, what with having to wade around in water almost up to their necks, so that at times they were even swimming. But it was no time to be squeamish, and every one of the boys meant business; so that in the end they had three doors anchored back of the shaky building.

They looked only a poor apology for boats, and no wonder the girls shuddered at the very idea of finding themselves afloat on the raging flood, with only a bobbing door to buoy them up.

Max was plainly worried. He admired the spirit which both Bessie and Mazie displayed when they declared that they would feel quite safe, if only the boys kept swimming alongside, to direct the floats toward the shore; at the same time he realized what tremendous difficulty they would have to keep the doors from "turning turtle," for there were many cunning eddies in the flood, that would strive to baffle their best efforts.

Besides, the girls would quickly find themselves wet through, and altogether the prospect was a pitiable one. Again and again did Max try to conceive of a better plan. He even went prowling around down below again, hoping to make some little discovery that would turn out to be of benefit to the three girls; but when he once more rejoined the others on the roof his face failed to announce any success.

Still Max did not allow himself to show signs of anything bordering on despair. In the first place the boy was not built that way, and had always shown a decided disposition to hold out to the very last gasp, as every fellow should, no matter how fortune frowns down on him. Then again Max understood that his face and his manner were bound to be considered a barometer by the others; who would be sure to gauge the prospects for a safe landing by what they saw reflected in his demeanor.

For this reason, if no other, Max forced himself to smile once in a while, and to assume a confident manner that he was far from feeling.

The question now seemed to be in connection with their leaving their perch. Of course they were better off on the roof than could possibly be the case once it had to be abandoned; but there was also the possibility of a sudden collapse on the part of the farm-house to be taken into consideration.

Max would not like to have this happen while the girls were still crouching on the shingled roof; because there could be no telling what would happen, once the building began to roll onward with the flood. All of them might be pitched headlong into the water, and it would be a difficult thing for them to save Mazie and the other two girls. Besides, the anchored doors might be lost, and though only makeshifts for boats, these were bound to be much better than nothing to help keep the helpless ones afloat.

The water must be rising still; at least it seemed to be coming against the exposed side of the partly submerged building with greater energy than before, Max was certain. The waves would strike the wall, and leap upward as though eager to engulf those who were just beyond their reach; so it seemed to the frightened girls at the time; though their terror would undoubtedly have been much greater but for the presence, and the inspiring words uttered by the boys.

There seemed nothing else to be done but embark, dangerous though that undertaking must prove. Max hated to announce this dictum to the girls, for he could easily understand what a fresh source of alarm it must cause to sweep over them. They had already gone through so much, calculated to inspire terror in their hearts, that any addition looked like rank cruelty; and yet what other solution could there be to the problem?

Just then Max and his chums would have gladly given every cent they had in the bank—and it was quite a goodly sum, for they had received rewards on account of certain services performed, as well as sold the pearls found in the fresh water mussels for a fine price—if they could only have been able to secure any kind of a boat capable of transporting those helpless ones safely to land. At another time they would have probably been more particular, and demanded a high-powered motor launch; or at the least one of those Cailie Outboard Motors to clamp on the stern of a rowboat; but right now it was a case of "my kingdom, not for a horse, but any sort of boat capable of floating."

Max heaved a sigh. He felt that he might as well wish to be given wings with which to fly ashore, as a boat. What few there were along the Evergreen River under normal conditions must either have been swamped in the sudden rising of the waters, or else be kept busy succoring imperiled people who had been caught in their homes by the flood, and threatened with drowning.

Just then the sun peeped out from a rift in the clouds. Strange what a remarkable difference even a fugitive glimpse of the sun may have on people, after the king of the day has refused to shine for forty-eight hours, while the rains persist in descending.

Like magic everybody seemed to become more cheerful. Things lost some of their gloomy aspect; even the rushing water looked far less bleak and threatening when those slanting shafts of sunlight glinted across the moving flood.

"Now, I take it that's a good sign!" said Steve, who persisted in remaining as near to Bessie as he could, in all reason, considering that he was dripping wet, and certainly could not look very presentable; but fortunately Bessie had come to her senses now, and to her mind Steve never appeared to greater advantage, because she knew he was doing all this on account of his friendship for her.

Really Steve did not know at what minute the calamity might swoop down upon them, and he wanted to be handy so that he could look after Bessie. Max would take care that Mazie Dunkirk did not suffer; and the other two chums had been privately told to attend to the lame child, so that all were provided for.

"And I do believe there's going to be a rainbow over in the west!" exclaimed Bessie, showing considerable interest, which seemed a pretty good sign that hope was not lying altogether dead within her girlish heart.

"I'm glad of that," said Max; "not because it will help us any, but if the rain that was promised passes over, there'll be a chance of the flood going down sooner. In fact, I don't believe it's going to get much higher than it is now."

"You never can tell," Bandy-legs remarked, showing a strange lack of proper caution, though Max tried to catch his eye, and would have given his foot a vigorous kick had he only been closer; "it all depends on whether they got the rain up in the hills where most of the water that flows down our old river comes from."

"Well, let's hope they didn't get any, then," said Max, quickly, as he saw a slight look of new fear creeping across the faces of the listening girls; "and on the whole I think we've got a heap to be thankful for. As long as we're here we'll see to it that the girls are taken care of; and if we do have to go ashore, why, we can make a regular picnic out of it; and you fellows will have a chance to show how much you know about camping in the woods without making any preparations beforehand."

"I'd just like to do that same!" exclaimed Steve, bravely; "nothing would please me better than to make a camp-fire, build a bark shelter for the girls, forage through the surrounding country for something to cook, and prove to everybody's satisfaction that we knew our business as amateur woodsmen. Don't you say the same, Bandy-legs and Toby?"

"I sure do," replied the former, with considerable fervor, as the pleasant times spent in former camps seemed to flash before his mind; "but what ails Toby here, fellers; he's going to have a fit if he don't get out what's sticking in his throat! Look at him gasping for breath, would you? What's the matter, Toby; seen another sea serpent have you; or is it a hippopotamus this time; perhaps a twenty foot alligator. Here, give one of your whistles, and get a grip on yourself, Toby!"

And the stuttering boy, brought to his senses by the admonition of his chum, did actually pucker up his lips, emit a sharp little whistle, and then working the muscles of his face as though trying to make a grimace, managed to utter just one word, which however thrilled the balance of the shivering group through and through, for that word was the magical one:

"Boat!"

CHAPTER X

"ALL ABOARD!"

"Where away?" cried Steve, with his customary impetuousness.

"Don't you dare fool us, Toby Jucklin!" exclaimed Bandy-legs, menacingly; for if the truth be told, he felt a twinge of envy because it had not been his sharp eyesight that had first detected the coming of a rescue party.

Max noticed just where Toby was pointing, and without wasting his breath in asking useless questions he applied himself to the task of ascertaining just how much truth there might be in the assertion.

Sure enough, he did manage to discover something that had the appearance of a boat; but as it rose and fell with the waves, now vanishing altogether from his sight, and then again being plainly seen, Max made it out to be a rowboat. There were no oars working in the sunlight, nor could he discover the first sign of life about the bobbing craft that was coming down on the flood.

"It is a boat, all right!" admitted Steve, presently, while all of them continued to stare eagerly at the advancing object; "but a derelict you might say, because there's not a sign of anybody aboard. And from the way she rolls so logy, I bet you she's half full of water right now."

The girls began to utter little plaintive exclamations.

"But notice that she floats all right, Steve," Max hastened to tell him; "and we'll soon find a way to empty that water out, if only we're lucky enough to lay our hands on that craft."

"But d'ye think it'll come this way?" asked Bandy-legs; "because I'm ready to swim out after it if there's any chance of the bloomin' old tub giving our crowd the go-by."

"We've got to get it, that's all," said Max, firmly; "I'd go after it myself if I thought it would miss hitting the house here. But let's watch, and see how that comes out. And, Bandy-legs, slip that noose at the end of the balance of the rope under your arms. If you do have to swim out to waylay the boat, we can pull you back again whether you get aboard or not."

"Now, that's a good idea, Max," Steve admitted. "It sure takes you to think up the right thing at the right time and place. I don't reckon there'll be such good luck as to be oars aboard a runaway boat; but even then it's going to be better for the girls than a floating door."

"Oh! I do hope you can get it then!" declared Bessie; and Steve hearing her say this felt as though he ought to be the one to have that noose fastened under his arms, rather than Bandy-legs, who could not swim quite as good.

There was intense excitement on the roof of the imperiled farm-house about that time. Every one of them seemed to be watching the coming of that bobbing object as though the fate of the world depended on its taking a direct course for the building standing alone in the flood.

"Seems like she was coming right along over the same course we did; how about that, Max?" called out Steve, presently, as the boat drew steadily closer to the fugitives of the wash-out.

"Yes, as nearly as I can decide that's what she's doing, Steve," Max replied.

"Oh! let's hope so," Mazie remarked, with a tremor in her voice, that told of quivering lips, and rapidly beating heart.

"Looky there!" burst out Bandy-legs just then; "if she ain't takin' a shoot this way even while we're sitting here wishing for the same to happen. I tell you she's going to hit the house ker-flop, too. No need of anybody jumpin' over and swimmin' out to her. But I'll leave the rope where it is, because I'll be in condition to roll off the roof, and grab her before she c'n slide past."

Nearer and nearer came the boat. It was easy to see that the craft was partly waterlogged, though still having her gunnels a considerable distance above the water. Either the boat leaked terribly, or else this water had splashed in from time to time as rougher places were encountered.

"Ready, Bandy-legs!" cried Max.

"Watch your eyes, old fellow!" warned Steve.

"And d-d-don't you l-l-let her g-g-get away on your l-l-life!" added Toby, who was greatly aroused, and had been edging down toward the gutter for several minutes now, evidently bound to be ready to lend a helping hand, if the other chum needed it.

It really seemed as though some unseen hand might be guiding that half swamped rowboat, in the interest of those who were so greatly in need of assistance; for it came heading in toward the house, urged on by the grip of the changing current, and finally actually bumped confidingly against the wall below the edge of the roof.

Bandy-legs was on the alert. He dropped over instantly, and they heard him utter a whoop of delight as he found himself actually in possession of a boat.

His first act was to slip the noose from under his arms, and his next to secure that end of the rope to the bow of the boat. Then he started in to make the water fly like everything, using his hat as a bailing bucket.

When he had to rest for a minute Bandy-legs stood up so that his head and shoulders came above the gutter of the roof, and grinned at the rest.

"How does she seem to be, Bandy-legs?" asked Steve.

"Course I can't just say for certain yet," came the reply; "but looks like our boat might be watertight, and that the waves have been splashing aboard all the time she's been adrift. Wait till I get the rest of the stuff out, and then I'll know for sure."

"How about oars?" asked Max.

"Ain't nary a sign of the same around, and I'm afraid they must a been washed overboard when—but hold on there, what's this I'm knocking against every time I dip deep? Say, here's luck in great big gobs, fellers; it's an oar stuck under the thwarts, as sure as you live! What, two of the same, seems like! Well, well, what do you know about that? Couldn't have asked for anything better, could we? Oh! don't I wish I had all this water out, though."

He had hardly spoken when some one else dropped into the boat, and started to hurling the water in great quantities over the side. It was Shack Beggs, and he had a tin basin in his hands. Max remembered having seen it floating around in the interior of the house, along with many other things; but at the time, as none of them wanted to take a wash, he had not bothered securing it. Shack must have remembered the basin, and realizing how well it might be utilized now as a bailing bucket, he had slipped through the scuttle and secured it.

The water began to go down rapidly under their united efforts; though a little kept coming in over the exposed side of the boat, as it rubbed against the wall of the farm-house.

Seeing this Max managed to help the other boys shift the location of their valued prize, and presently it was dangling alongside the three floating doors, no longer of any moment in their eyes.

"When will we go aboard?" asked Steve, as a more violent shiver passed over the doomed building than at any previous time.

"Right away," replied the other, who had felt his own heart stop beating for a brief space of time, as he actually feared that the catastrophe was about to overwhelm them.

"I'm willing, Max," said Mazie, trying to speak bravely.

"Then come, let me help you down; and the boys in the boat will be there to do their part; after which we'll get the other girls aboard," and saying this Max proceeded to give Mazie his hand, so that she might creep down the slope of the roof securely.

It was no easy task to manage things so that the three girls were all taken on board without any accident; but then Shack Beggs again proved himself invaluable, for it was his strong arms that held the boat close to the house while the transfer was being made. Max was secretly delighted with the way Shack was turning out. He actually believed there would be another vacancy in the ranks of that gang of young toughs in Carson after this; and was determined that if any friendly word or act of his could induce Shack to turn over a new leaf, they would certainly not be withheld. Presently all of them had embarked.

The water by how was well out of the boat, and so far as they could see not much more was coming in; and that could be readily handled, thanks to the possession of that dented basin which Shack had twisted into a handy scoop.

Max had fixed the rope so that by releasing one end it would allow the boat to drop down the stream with the swift current.

Steve had one oar and Bandy-legs the other, thrust out, and ready for use.

"Well, here's where we have to say good-bye to the French farm-house," and saying this Max let go the rope; "now, pull away, boys, and head for the shore!"

It had already been decided which bank they must aim to reach; there was really very little choice between them so far as nearness went; but the boys thought it would be wiser to make for the west shore. Carson lay on that side, and then the ground as a whole lay somewhat higher, so that once they landed they would be less liable to come across impassable sloughs and lagoons formed by the back-water of the flooded river.

Both rowers bent their backs, and the boat began to make progress. They had not been laboring in this fashion three minutes when Bessie gave utterance to a bubbling cry of anguish.

"Oh! see there what is happening to Uncle Asa's place!" she exclaimed.

The little lame girl set up a loud cry, and sobbed as though her heart would break, because that farm-house had been her home all her life; and it was now toppling over into the river.

They could see it moving, at first slowly, then with a sudden rush. It careened far on one side, and then surged to the other dreadfully. Had they still been clinging to the ridge the chances were that they would have been thrown into the water; and besides, there was always great danger that the house would fall to pieces before long.

"Well, we've got a whole lot to be thankful for, anyway!" Steve presently remarked, as he patted Bessie's, hand with one of his, using the oar with the other meanwhile.

"I should say we had!" declared Bandy-legs; "I'd rather be here in this bully old boat ten times over, to squattin' up on that old roof, seesawin' along every-which-way. Here, pull harder, Steve; you're lettin' her yaw around terrible. We want to head for the shore and not down-river way."

As the two rowers continued to work regularly they kept gradually nearing the western shore of the flood. Of course this was far removed from what the bank must be under ordinary conditions, in places as much as a quarter of a mile further inland. The water was sweeping through the lower branches of trees that all their lives had been far removed from the influence of the river; and there would be many changes in the aspect of things when the flood eventually subsided.

The girls sat there silent, and absorbed in watching the dizzy evolutions of the drifting farmhouse that was rapidly passing away from them down-stream. Of course it meant more to the lame child than any one else, and Max could feel sorry for her. He had only to put himself in her place, to realize the sadness that would be sure to overwhelm him should he watch his loved home carried off, never to be seen again.

However he had many other things to think of, and could not spend any time in crying over spilt milk. Nothing they could do would mend matters so far as saving the French home was concerned; and they had enough to do in looking out for their own safety.

"If you get tired, let some of the rest of us spell you, boys," Max was saying to the pair of rowers, who had all they could do to stem the furious current that every now and then caught them in a pocket, from which they could only drag the boat by desperate labor; "I'm a good hand with the oar, and I know Shack is a regular crackerjack at the business. Just say the word when you get played out, and we'll change places with you."

Shack shot him a grateful look. It seemed as though he appreciated what Max had said, and which seemed to place him on the same level as the rest of the fellows. Somehow Shack was feeling differently from any time in the past; why, all this business of getting soaked through, and battling with the flood was in the nature of a picnic to him, accustomed to rubbing up against hard knocks as he was. And it felt pretty nice to be looked on as a "comrade" by these fellows whom he had always fought tooth and nail in the past; much nicer than loafing with that old crowd once led by Ted Shatter but now under the guidance of Ossie Kemp.

They had struck another bad place in the flood, where cross currents made it difficult work rowing. Both boys strained themselves to the utmost to resist the grip of the stream. Once across this section, and possibly they would have it easier all the way to the shore.

Steve was working with his accustomed fits and starts. He would allow things to go against him, for a short interval, and then throwing on all his reserve power into the breach make his oar fairly bend with the furious strain he put upon it.

Suddenly there was a sharp snap. One of the girls gave a cry; it was Bessie, for she had been watching Steve at the time, and saw instantly what had happened.

Indeed, it was manifest to every one, because Steve almost took a "crab" by falling backwards. His sudden splurge had been too much for the strength of the oar he was handling; and it had broken in two!

The catastrophe staggered them all for the moment; because they could readily understand what it would mean; since with but one oar they could hardly expect to continue rowing the boat to the shore, still some little distance away.

CHAPTER XI

GOOD CHEER BY THE CAMP FIRE

Toby made a quick lurch, and managed to snatch up the broken blade of Steve's now useless oar. As they had no way of mending it, tin, nails, or hammer, it was next-door to useless to them.

Already that fierce current was seizing them in its remorseless grip; and the overloaded boat began to spin down-stream, turning around and around in its helplessness.

"Gee! whiz! what can we do now, Max?" asked Bandy-legs, ready to jump overboard if the other but said the word, and urge the boat toward the shore by swimming on his back.

Before Max could frame a reply something happened. Shack leaned forward from toward the stern and took the oar from the hands of Bandy-legs.

"Let me show yuh how tuh do it!" he said, not roughly at all, but eagerly, as though just too well pleased to have it in his power to assist.

Max understood what he meant to do; in fact, he had been about to suggest the very same remedy for their ills when Shack made his move.

"There's a sculling hole in the back of the stern seat, Shack!" he called out, being more up in the bow himself.

The oar upon being fitted in the cavity could be rapidly turned to the right and to the left, with a peculiar motion known to those who have learned the art of successfully sculling a craft in this way. It is wonderful what progress can be made in that fashion. Shack seemed to know all about it, for presently Bandy-legs emitted a whoop that would have shamed an Indian brave.

"Say, you're making her just walk along, Shack, that's right!" he exclaimed.

"And that oar going bad didn't knock us out at all, did it?" demanded Steve, who felt sorely distressed because it had been his bungling way of rowing that had brought about their trouble, and with Bessie on board too, which cut him worse than anything else.

"Seems like it wouldn't," Max told him, feeling quite satisfied himself.

Shack kept working away like a good fellow, and the boat drew closer and closer to the shore all the time. There was now no reason to believe that they would have any more trouble in landing; and Max began to take closer notice of the shore than he had up to that time done.

"None of us have ever been as far down the river as this," he remarked; "I know I haven't, anyway."

"I was down once years ago, and saw the big falls where we might have taken a header if we'd kept drifting," Bandy-legs explained; "but say, I don't seem to remember the first thing about the country. You could lose me down here without any trouble, I guess. Plenty of forest all right, eh, Max; and we won't have any great time makin' a fire, if only we get matches? Mine are all wet."

"I carry a few in a waterproof case," Max told him; "so don't let that worry you any, Bandy-legs. The question is with us, after the fire, what? We'll all be hungry and the girls haven't had a bite to eat since early morning."

"Well, there's a house, surrounded by water," suggested Steve; "guess we'll have to cabbage anything we can find around loose. In times like this you can't wait to ask permission. Eat first, and pay for it afterwards, that's the motto we'll have to go by. If we're on the right side of the luck fence we might even run across a smoked ham hangin' from the rafters. They keep all kinds of good things sometimes in these cabins along the shore."

"Seems to be something like a hencoop back of the house," added Bandy-legs.

"Oh! s-s-say, don't go to g-g-getting a feller's m-m-mouth all made up for nice r-r-roast chicken, and then never find any," objected Toby.

"Course we'll find all sorts of good things," declared Bandy-legs, stoutly; "why, look what's happened to us already; and tell me that this ain't our lucky day. We went down with the old bridge, but not one of us got thrown into the water. Then we sailed twenty miles, and dropped in on the roof of the French house just like we'd been drawn by a magnet, which p'raps some of us must a been, hey, Steve? And then, by George! just when we wanted a boat the worst ever, along came this tub, and heading straight in for our shaky roost like it was being piloted by hands none of us could see. Luck? Why, we've got it plastered all over us, from head to foot. Chickens, ham, anything you want, just ask for it, and then wait and have faith!"

"We're glad that you feel so certain," Mazie told him, "because I'm ready to own up that I'm awfully hungry, and could eat almost anything just now."

"And I'm beginning to feel a little weak myself," admitted Bessie; "which, I suppose, is caused from going without any regular meal. None of us dared go back down through that trap once we got on the roof, because we were afraid the house might float off while we were below. Yes, we hope there will be something you can get in that house."

"Seems to be abandoned, all right," Steve remarked, shading his eyes with his hands in order to see better.

"There's somebody over on the bank beyond, and as near as I can make out it's an old woman," Max told them just at that point; "perhaps she's guarding some of the stuff that was saved from the cabin when the water came up around it; while her man has gone to get a horse and wagon, or a boat."

"Well, we're going to land here," Bandy-legs ventured; "and it won't be hard to go up and interview the old lady. P'raps we can make a bargain with her for some of her grub. I've got a dollar along with me, and I reckon some of the rest ought to make as good a showing."

"There'll be no trouble about that part of it, if only the food is around," Max assured them. "If the worst comes we'll have to commandeer the food market, and settle afterwards. Can you make it all right, Shack?"

"Easy as fallin' off a log," replied the stout boy, who was still wielding the sculling oar back and forth with that peculiar turning motion that presented the broad surface of the blade to the water all the time, and induced the boat to move forward with a steady action.

He made his words good a few minutes later, for the stem of the boat ran gently up against the bank, where a log offered a good chance for disembarking.

No one would want a better landing stage; and so the three girls managed to go ashore without wetting their feet any more than they had been before.

Every one seemed glad to get on solid ground again. Even Max secretly admitted that it did feel very good to know he had no longer to depend on the whims of the current, but could go wherever he willed.

"Let's hunt out a decent place to make a camp," he remarked, "and then after we get the shelter started, and the cheery fire warming things up, two of us ought to wander off up the bank and see what's doing around that house."

"I'll go with yon, Max," said Bandy-legs hastily, as though more or less afraid that he might come in a poor second, as it was a case of "first come, first served."

They drew the boat well up, and fastened it with the length of rope that served as a painter; the clothes-line Max thought to take along with him, as there was a possibility they might need it before through with this adventure.

Then they started through the woods, which just at this point happened to be unusually dense, with great trees rearing their crests a hundred feet or so above the heads of the shipwrecked Crusoes.

It was not long before Max called attention to a certain spot which he claimed would answer all their present needs.

"There's plenty of stuff to make a shelter of brush and branches with," he observed, "though it would be easier all around if we had a hatchet along."

"That's right," added Steve; "and if I'd only had any idea that old bridge was going to dump us all into the drink the way it did I'd have had lots of things fixed different, give you my affidavy I would. But we ought to be able to work a fairly decent brush shanty without. It won't be the first we've put up, and I certainly hope it isn't goin' to be the last, either."

Filled with this winning spirit the boys quickly busied themselves. Shack gathered brush with the rest, and really did more than his share of the work. This was right in his element, and no one had to tell him how to proceed.

Max waited to see things progressing before he started off. A fire had already been started, and the cheery flames did much toward dispelling the feeling of gloom that had begun to gnaw at their hearts. There is nothing in the world better calculated to dissipate worry and liven things up than a genuine camp-fire. It seems to dissipate doubt, give the heart something to grip, and in every way make the prospect brighter.

After escaping from the flood without any serious damage they were all full of enthusiasm now. Even the two older girls insisted on helping later on; if only food could be procured the boys must let them do all the cooking. That was only a fair distribution of the labor; it was what happened in Indian camps, with the warriors securing game, and the squaws preparing the meals.

Presently Max, catching the eye of Bandy-legs, crooked his finger, and made a significant gesture with his head. The other understood just what was in the wind for he dropped the armful of fuel he happened at the time to be carrying toward the fire, and hastened to reach the side of the leader.

Max knew that just then they could not think of walking any distance in order to seek aid. The day was pretty well along, and as more rain might come with the night, it seemed the part of prudence that they prepare in advance to meet further trials. If only they managed to come across something that could be made to do for a supper, all else could for the time being be forgotten.

"We're off, Steve," Max called out, after he had waved his hand in the direction of the girl whose eyes followed him wherever he went; "you three keep right along as you're doing now. Make the shack as snug as you can; and if it'll shed water, so much the better; though I don't think we're going to get any more rain just at present."

Bandy-legs was at his side, and together they strode away. It was no great task to keep heading up-stream, because they had frequent glimpses of the heaving surface of the flood, which was ever at their right, because they had landed on the western shore, and were heading north at the time.

"Thought I heard dogs abarkin' just then," observed Bandy-legs, who had good ears as well as sharp eyes.

"Yes, I did too, but somewhere away up on the wooded hills there. Like as not this flood has chased plenty of dogs away from their homes, and they may be running in packs, hunting something to eat."

"Huh! hope we don't happen to run foul of a pack then," Bandy-legs insinuated; "and for fear that we do I'm going to be ready."

With that he picked up a rather stout cudgel which he swung a few times as if to accustom his arm to the motion.

Apparently Max did not think there was any particular reason for alarm. He must have figured that the dogs they had heard were hunting game a mile or two back in the woods, and that there was little chance of their coming closer to the river.

"I can see the house ahead there," he announced five minutes later.

"Yes, and it's surrounded by water too," added his chum; "no wonder the folks got out and left; they'd be silly to stay till it was too late. Why, that cabin might be carried off any time like the other house was, even if it ain't so far out I reckon we must have drifted half a mile further down when we kept rowing so hard; because that was a stiff current, believe me."

"Fully half a mile, Bandy-legs," Max assured him, and then fell to craning his neck in the endeavor to locate the woman they believed they had seen among the trees at a point where the water ended.

Two minutes later and Max uttered a satisfied exclamation.

"I see the woman," he told his companion, "and just as we thought she's an old person, bent over considerably. Perhaps she couldn't go far away after she had to quit her house; perhaps she's nearly as helpless as the crippled French child. If it wasn't for Mabel being unable to walk we might be trying to find shelter back in the country right now. Come on and we'll interview her. She may be glad to go with us, and spend the night in camp; it would be good for her and the girls would like it too."

The old woman had seen their approach. She looked anything but happy, and Max really began to believe that the poor soul stood in danger of losing all she owned in the wide world, if her little cabin went out with the flood.

"How do you do, ma'm?" he said, cheerily, as he and his chum came up. "We're all from the town of Carson. The bridge went out, and we were on it at the time. It carried five of us down to where the French farm-house was standing, half under water, and there we found three girls on the roof, two of them friends of ours from town. A boat happened to drift within reach, and we have come ashore. But as Asa French's little daughter, Mabel, is lame and weak the chances are we'll have to camp in the woods for the night, and go for help in the morning. Now, wouldn't you like to join us to-night, because it'll be a lonely time for you here, and it may start in and rain again? We want to get something to eat the worst kind, and have money to buy whatever you happen to have handy, chickens, ham, potatoes or anything at all. The girls are nearly starved they say. Now how about it, ma'm?"

The little old woman had listened to him talking with a sparkle of interest in her eyes. Apparently she admired the lad from the very start. Bandy-legs was hardly prepossessing enough to hope to make a favorable impression on a stranger at first sight; you had to know the boy with the crooked legs in order to appreciate his good qualities; but Max won friends by the score even before they understood how clever he could be.

"You're perfectly welcome to anything you can find in my cabin, providing that you can get out there, and secure it," the little old woman told them. "Perhaps you might manage with the aid of the boat. And I believe I'll accept your kind invitation to accompany you back to your camp. I'm accustomed to being by myself, but inside a house, not out in the open woods, and on the brink of a dreadful flood. So consider it a bargain, son. Show me the way to get there, and after that it may pay you to bring your boat up so as to reach my little house out there surrounded by water."

CHAPTER XII

THE WILD DOG PACK

This prospect pleased the two boys very much. Max believed that they could manage to drag the boat up along the shore, and then scull out to where the house stood, surrounded by water.

Accordingly they first of all led the old woman to where the others were making as comfortable a camp as the meager conditions allowed. It turned out that the little lame girl, Mabel French, knew her very well, and addressed her as Mrs. Jacobus. She took occasion to tell Max aside that the old lady had lived alone for many years, but that instead of being poor as she seemed, in reality people said she was very rich, only eccentric. Perhaps she had a history, Max thought, as he looked at the wrinkles on her face, and noticed the kindly eyes, and wanted to hide her pain away from a cruel world.

He and Bandy-legs proceeded to drag the boat up to a point above the cabin, and then pushing out, headed for their goal. The current was fully as swift as before, but as they had taken all proper precautions they did not have a great deal of difficulty in making it.

Once they had secured their boat by the kitchen door, and they entered, wading with the water up to their waists. As soon as they had entered Bandy-legs gave a wild cheer.

"Great governor! look at the fine ham hanging from the rafters, with strings of garlic, and all sorts of things!" he cried out. "You rummage around in closets, Max, while I'm climbing up, and grabbing that same smoked pork. Say, the country is saved, and those poor girls can have something worth while to eat. I've learned a new way to fry ham without even a pan; though chances are we'll be able to pick up something along that line in the kitchen here."

They did, and all sorts of other things besides, which Max fancied the girls could make use of, and which were really in danger of being lost, if the cabin was carried away. He rooted in every cupboard, secured a lot of dishes and tinware, knives, forks and spoons, even a loaf of bread and some cake that he found in a japanned tin box high up on the shelf of a closet, coffee, sugar, and condensed milk, butter, potatoes, onions and a lot of other things too numerous to mention, but which attracted the attention of the hungry boys.

Bandy-legs was fairly bubbling over with delight, and kept declaring that it was the greatest picnic ever known. All the perils of the past had apparently vanished from his mind, and he was as happy as any one could be over the prospect of enjoying a regular camp meal by the glow of a jolly woods fire.

"Guess we'd better hold up about now, Max," he went on to say, when they had piled the stuff in the boat until it looked as though moving day had come around again, or an eviction was in progress.

"You're right there, Bandy-legs, because if we kept on much more there wouldn't be standing room for the two of us, and you'd have to swim alongside. So let's call it a day's work and quit. Besides, we'll have our hands full getting our stuff ashore. You stand ready to spell me if I play out, will you?"

"I'd like to have a chance at that sculling racket, anyhow, Max; never took a turn at the same, and so you'd better let me try it when we get in closer to shore."

"Only too glad to fix you up," replied the other, as he started to work.

It turned out all right, and they managed to reach land about as close to the spot where the camp had been pitched as it was possible to get. When the two came staggering along, laden down with all sorts of stuff, there was a whoop from Steve and Toby, who stopped work on the shack to run and help them.

"Well, this is great shakes, for a fact!" exclaimed the former, as he relieved Max of a part of his load; "I declare if you haven't fetched enough junk to fit us up in housekeeping for a year. And I guess the little old lady won't be sorry, either, because p'raps you've been and saved some of her property that would have gone floating down the river to-night."

Mrs. Jacobus smiled and nodded her head when she saw what the boys had found.

"I had that fowl killed and dressed yesterday, meaning to make a dinner off it to-day, but the coming of the flood took all thought of eating out of my head," she remarked, as Bandy-legs exposed the featherless bird, which had been found hanging from a beam, just like the ham and other things.

There was great rejoicing in the camp. Bessie and Mazie immediately took charge of all the stuff that had been brought ashore. If they wanted any assistance they called on one of the boys, as happened when the ham was to be sliced. Fortunately Max had secured a large knife in the kitchen, and with this he managed splendidly, cutting around the bone, as they lacked a saw.

Mrs. Jacobus had told the boys where there were some stray boards lying in the woods not far away, and already the shack builders had paid several visits to the pile, returning each time dragging spoils after them. These they could use to splendid advantage in their work, and when the shelter was finally completed it promised to be amply large enough for the three girls and Mrs. Jacobus, to keep them from the night air. Should it storm possibly all of them could crawl under, though the boys declared they meant to keep the camp-fire burning throughout the night, and would not need anything over them.

"Things are looking some different from what they did while we were drifting along on that wobbly old piece of the broken bridge, eh, fellows?" Steve wanted to know, as later on, when it began to grow dim with the approach of night, the boys sat down to rest, and watch their force of cooks getting supper ready.

"Couldn't be a bigger change anyway you fix it," assented Bandy-legs; "and let me tell you these girls certainly know how to go at things the right way. Now, as I've been taking lessons from our cook, Nora, I ought to be considered something of a judge, and I want to say right here that I never whiffed more appetizing smells around a camp-fire in all my born days than are filling the air this very minute. I don't see how I can stand it much longer; seems that I'm possessed with a wild desire to jump up and begin eating like a cannibal."

"Well, don't you pick out Bessie when you do," Steve warned him solemnly; "she may be sweet enough to eat, but not for you, Bandy-legs. But just think how the girls must suffer getting all these rations ready, and not having had a mouthful of food since breakfast-time while all the rest of us had lunch at noon."

"Max, you said you had a bell somewhere, so please ring it, because everything's ready," Mazie called out just at that minute.

Whereupon Max picked up an extra skillet that had come with the other kitchen stuff, and pounded on it loud and long with a great big stick; while the rest of the party hastened to find places around the makeshift camp table, formed out of some of the best boards, laid on the ground, because they had neither hammer nor nails with which to construct a real table.

It was a merry sight to see them all, and much laughing was indulged in. Young hearts may not long stay depressed; and the loss of Mr. French's home, while it may have seemed too bad in the eyes of all of them, was not irreparable, since he was considered well-to-do, and later on could build a newer and better house in place of the one swept away.

No lives had been lost, and hence there was really no occasion for them to pull long faces and make themselves miserable.

Mrs. Jacobus was smiling all the while. This was evidently a new as well as novel experience with the little old lady who had lived alone so many years. She could hardly take her eyes off the face of Max, she seemed so greatly interested in the boy; and the three girls also had a share of her attention. Perhaps after this she might make somewhat of a change in her mode of living; she had discovered that there were people worth knowing in this dreary world, after all; and that it was foolish to hide away from everybody, just because of some bitter stroke of fortune away back in the past.

Steve was the life of the party. He felt so overjoyed because of the kind fate that had allowed him to be of considerable use to Bessie French, so that their old friendship was renewed, this time to remain, that he seemed to be fairly bubbling over with spirits. He made witty remarks about most of the food they had, and kept the others laughing from the beginning of the meal until it reached its conclusion, with the dishes well cleaned out.

Everybody had an abundance, and the boys seemed never to weary of declaring how glad they were to have the proper kind of cooks along. Their own style of camp cookery might do in an emergency, when they were cast upon their own resources; but it lacked something or other that a girl somehow seemed to know instinctively how to put in it, and make all the difference imaginable in the taste.

Steve even volunteered to favor them with a song, and it would have required very little encouragement to have extended this to a dance, so light-hearted was he feeling. No one would ever have believed that this was the same Steve whose face had been long-drawn with anxiety only a comparatively few hours back, while they were drifting on the swift current of the flood, with their strange craft in danger of going to pieces at any moment, and leaving them struggling in the wilderness of rushing water.

There were some other things that wise Max had secured from the abandoned cottage of Mrs. Jacobus. These had been left down by the boat, and when he presently walked over that way, and came back laden down with blankets there was a loud cheer from the other boys, accompanied by much hand-clapping from the girls.

"Why, this is just delightful," Mazie told him, after he had first of all made her choose the best blanket, which she immediately turned over to the crippled child, taking another for her own individual use; "and if we'd only known how nice it was all going to come out, you can be sure none of us would have allowed ourselves to cry as we sat there on the roof waiting to be drowned. We'll never forget this experience, will we, Bessie?"

"I should say not," came the prompt answer; "and the boys have done themselves proud through it all. Just to think of their being on that bridge when it fell into the flood, and none of them even thrown into the river. I never heard of such great good fortune. And then to be taken straight to where we were hoping and praying for some one to come along and save us. Well, after this I'm not going to be so silly as to doubt it any longer."

"What?" asked Steve, quickly, but in a low voice.

"Oh! just that there must be a sweet little cherub aloft watching over me," she replied, giving him a saucy look.

"I thought you might mean that it was wicked for people to quarrel, and that it never could happen again between two persons that I know," Steve went on to say.

"Well, perhaps I did mean that too; but no matter, I've seen a great light, and sitting there on that terrible roof so many hours was a good thing for me, Steve. I'm never going to be such a spitfire again; and I'll never condemn anybody unheard, I give you my word. But what's the matter with you, Bessie; you are shaking like a leaf. I hope you haven't taken cold."

"No, it isn't that, Mazie," replied the other Carson girl; "but listen to the horrid wolves up there on the hill; and it seems to give me a bad feeling when I get to thinking of what would happen if they should come down here and attack us, when we haven't a single gun to defend ourselves with."

Bandy-legs started chuckling.

"Wolves don't yelp like that, Bessie," he remarked; "what you hear is a pack of wild dogs hunting something to eat. Since the water got so high, like as not they haven't had their meals as regular as they'd like, since lots of places are flooded out; so they've got together, and are rampaging around in search of grub. They do seem to be making a regular circus up there; and Max, I believe they're workin' down this way."

"Oh! dear! then this camping out isn't such great sport as it seemed!" cried pretty Bessie French, looking appealingly toward Steve, as though she expected him as her knight to stand between should any danger threaten.

"I was thinking that myself, Bandy-legs," Max admitted; "it may be that their keen scent has gotten wind of the smell from our cooking supper at last, and started them this way, bent on making a raid on our stores."

"Whatever can we do?" entreated Mazie, looking to Max to get them out of this new difficulty, for as everybody knew he always had a plan ready.

"If they should come this way you girls would have to climb up among the lower branches of this tree here," said Max. "You could make it without the least trouble, and keep out of reach of the dogs' teeth. Do you understand that, Mazie, Bessie, Mabel? Yes, and you too, Mrs. Jacobus."

The old lady took something out of her pocket and carefully handed it over to Max. To his astonishment he discovered that he was holding a brand new automatic quick-firing revolver of the latest pattern. Undoubtedly then Mrs. Jacobus, while living alone, had not taken any chances. Tramps or dogs might molest her, and she probably meant to be in a condition to defend herself. Perhaps, too, she may have carried quite a good-sized amount of money about her person, and wished to be in a condition to keep yeggmen from robbing her by day or by night.

Somehow the feel of the weapon gave Max a sensation of renewed confidence. With such a reliable tool he fancied that there would be little cause for anxiety, even should that pack of snapping hungry dogs dash into the camp, seeking to raid their larder, and ready to attack them if prevented from carrying out their design.

"Get hold of clubs, boys, if you can find them!" he told the others; "because the yelping and barking is certainly coming straight this way, and we'd better be ready to beat them off if they try to rob us. Anything that will make an impression will do; and when you strike, do it with vim!"

"Will we?" cried Steve, who still had a splendid club he had picked up some time back; "just let me get a single whack at a dog, I don't care what his breed or size or color, and his name will be Dennis, or Mud, I don't know which. But just as you said, Max, they are coming this way full tilt. Whew! sounds like there might be a round dozen in the bunch, and from a yapping ki-yi to a big Dane, with his heavy bark like the muttering of thunder."

"Leave that big one to me, remember," said Max; "and you fellows look after the smaller fry. We'll have to show them that because they're running loose and in a pack, they don't own the woods by a long shot. Now, climb up into that tree, girls, because they'll be here in a minute or so, I'm afraid!"

CHAPTER XIII

THE DEFENCE OF THE CAMP

"Mabel first, please, Max!" said Mazie, as all of them hastened over to the tree that had been selected as the harbor of refuge on account of the fact that its lower branches seemed to invite an ascent.

Max gave Steve a knowing nod, and the two of them quickly whisked the little lame French girl up in the first crotch like magic.

Before Mazie really knew what they were going to do she was following after the first climber; and as they made room for the others, first Mrs. Jacobus, and then last of all Bessie found lodgment there.

"If you can manage to get up a little higher it would be safer all around," Max told them, though he tried his best not to alarm the girls by intimating that the lower limb of the tree might still be within jumping distance of an agile hound.

Immediately after performing his duty Steve picked up his club again. Meanwhile the other three boys had brushed around and armed themselves with the most available weapons the dead wood afforded. Bandy-legs was fortunate in having one already to his suiting, and the others did the best they could; so that there was quite a formidable assortment of cudgels swinging back and forth as the owners tested their capacity for mischief; much as the intending batter at a critical stage of a baseball game may be seen to practice with two clubs before stepping up to the plate.

There could no longer be any doubt as to the speedy coming of the dog pack, as their eager yelps and barks sounded very close. It must have been that in their hungry condition they had picked up the odor of food far away, because a dog's sense of smell is remarkably acute, especially when half starved.

Max only waited in order to throw plenty of dry fuel on the fire before joining the battle line. If they were compelled to put up a stiff fight in order to keep their food supply intact, he knew that they would need all the light they could get, because with the coming of night, darkness had settled upon the forest lining the western bank of the flooded river.

"Whee! listen to the way they're tearing along, would you?" exclaimed Bandy-legs, as the noise drew rapidly nearer.

Every fellow seemed to take in a big breath. It was as though he meant to nerve himself for the exciting times to follow.

"Remember, leave the biggest dog to me!" Max told them, desirous of impressing this fact upon their minds; for with that powerful little automatic pistol in his possession, handed over to him by the owner of the abandoned cabin, he felt much better able to cope with a monster Dane or a huge mastiff than any of those who simply carried sticks might have been.

Max did not fancy the job before him. He had always confessed to a great liking for dogs of almost all kinds, and the thought of being compelled to shoot one, even in self-defense, did not appeal to him; though it was a grim necessity that forced him to contemplate such a massacre.

These animals having been shut off from their regular food supply because of the flood that had driven their masters from home, were only following out the dictates of their natures, in seeking to satisfy the demands of hunger. Under ordinary conditions they may have been the most desirable of companions, and valued highly by those who owned them.

There was no other way to meet the emergency save by dispersing the savage pack. And Max knew that the animal of the heavy bark must be a powerful brute, capable of inflicting serious damage to any one upon whom he descended; hence he must in some way manage to dispose of the beast before he could leap on his intended prey.

"I see 'em!" suddenly almost shrieked Bandy-legs; and all of the boys might have echoed his announcement, for they caught sight of a confused scrambling mass approaching at a furious pace.

This almost immediately developed into separate units, as the dogs rushed directly into the camp. Max could see that there were no two alike, and in the lead was a mastiff as large as any wolf that ever followed in the wake of a wounded stag, a tawny colored animal, with wide-open jaws that must have filled the watching girls with a sense of abject horror, even though they were apparently safe from attack up among the branches of the tree.

Max had eyes for no other after that. Let his chums and Shack Beggs take care of the New Foundland, the Irish setter, the beagle, the rabbit hound, and several more, even to a sturdy looking squatty bulldog that must have used his short bowlegs to some advantage to keep pace with the rest of the pack; his duty was to meet the oncoming of that natural leader, and wind up his career.

The five boys had stationed themselves partly in front of the shelter where all of their food supplies had been placed, though at the same time they stood between the tree and the rushing dogs.

Straight at them the pack went, helter-skelter. It may not have been so much a desire to attack human beings that animated the animals as the keen sense of smell telling them that provisions were to be found back in that rustic shack.

Max waited until the big leader was almost upon them before he started to use his automatic. Indeed, one of the girls in the tree, gasped his name in terror, under the impression that Max may have been so petrified with astonishment at sight of the size of the mastiff that he could not pull the trigger of his weapon.

But it was not so, and Steve, who was alongside, knew it full well, because he could hear Max saying steadily all the while:

"Hold firm, boys; don't get rattled! I've got that big thief potted! Steady now, everybody; and hit the line hard!"

That was the encouraging way Max used to call out to his players on the high school eleven when they were fighting for victory on the gridiron with a rival school. It did much to nerve those who heard; and Steve especially needed some such caution to keep him from springing to meet the coming attack halfway.

Then there sounded a peculiar snapping report. It was the automatic doing its duty. Firm was the hand that gripped the little weapon, and unflinching the eye back of the same.

A shriek from the tree told that the girls were watching every move in the exciting game that was being played. The mastiff was seen to stop in his headlong rush, and roll over in a heap; then he struggled to his feet again, only to have another flash directed into his eyes; and this time Max must have made sure work of it, because the huge animal did not attempt to rise again.

Meanwhile the rest of the pack had continued its forward progress, and as those waiting clubs began to swing and play there was a confused exchange of shouts, yaps and yelps that must have filled a listener's heart with wonder, providing he did not know the meaning of the fracas.

Deprived of the dominating spirit of their leader, and met with such a furious bombardment at the hands of the four boys, the balance of the pack could not hold out long. Their hunger did not seem to be equal to their fear of those clubs striking with such tremendous vim that in many cases the victim was hurled completely over. The attack became weaker and weaker; first one animal went howling away completely cowed, and then another took flight, until presently the bulldog was the only one left.

He had managed to seize Toby's club and was holding on with a death grip, straining his best to pull the same out of the hands of the owner. Steve was for turning on him, and belaboring the beast with his own cudgel; but Max, who knew the nature of the beast better than any of the others, felt sure that this sort of treatment would only result in a general fight, and that in the end the animal would either have to be shot, or else he must bite one of them seriously.

"Wait!" he called out; "keep back, the rest of you, and leave him to me!"

Thinking of course that he meant to advance, and use his firearm in order to finish the stubborn bulldog, the three other boys backed away, leaving only Toby standing there, holding one end of his club, while the canine enemy maintained that savage grip on the other, and sought to wrest it away.

But Max had had enough of dog killing for one night, and meant to try other tactics in this case. He dodged into the shelter, and almost immediately reappeared bearing with him some food that had been left over, scraps of bread and fragments from their supper.

These he tossed close to the nose of the stubborn bulldog, while the rest of the party watched to see the result. Would hunger prevail, or the disposition to continue fighting cause the animal to keep on chewing the end of Toby's club?

Presently they saw the unwelcome visitor begin to sniff eagerly. Then he suddenly released those terrible teeth of his, the iron jaw relaxed, and the next thing they knew the ferocious bulldog was devouring the food Max had thrown down, with every symptom of satisfaction.

Max went back and secured more of the same kind.

"We can get plenty, once we leave here in the morning," he told Bandy-legs when the latter showed a disposition to murmur against the seeming extravagance; "and I'd hate to kill that dog. I'm sure from his looks he must be of fine stock, and worth a heap to his owner. Besides, I've knocked one over, and that's one too many to please me. Now watch what I'll do."

With that he approached, and offered the dog the rest of the food. In another minute he could have patted the heretofore savage beast on the back, only that Max was too wise to trouble a feeding dog.

"Nothing more to be feared from him, I guess," remarked Steve, who had watched all this with distended eyes; "you know dogs from the ground up,

Max. But do you think it's safe to have that terror around? The girls won't want to come down out of the tree while he's in camp."

"You're mistaken there," said Bessie, as she dropped beside him; "I'm not at all afraid of dogs when they're natural; and besides, I know this fine fellow quite well. He belongs to a neighbor of my uncle, and he used to come to me as though he rather liked me; didn't you, Bose?"

At mention of his name the ferocious looking bulldog with the bowed legs actually wagged his crooked stub of a tail, and gave the girl a look. As he was now through feeding, and seemed to be in a contented frame of mind, Bessie continued to talk to him in a wheedling way; and presently was able to slip a hand upon his head, though it gave Steve a cold chill to see her do it.

Max had meanwhile dragged the other dog out of sight in the bushes, though Toby had to help him, such was the size of the wretched mastiff that had been brought to a bad end through his hunger, and a determination to raid the camp of the flood fugitives.

The balance of the pack had apparently been taught a severe lesson, and would not return again. Their barking continued to be heard at intervals throughout the night, but always at a considerable distance.

As it was so very uncomfortable up in the tree, and the bulldog seemed to have made up his mind to be friendly with those who had kindly attended to his wants, Mazie, the lame girl, and Mrs. Jacobus finally consented to be helped down. They kept suspicious eyes on the four-legged visitor however, and insisted that Bose be rigorously excluded from the rustic shelter under which they soon purposed seeking their rest.

Max finally managed to rig up a collar, which was attached to the rope, and Bessie secured this around the dog's neck, after which Bose was anchored to another tree.

He must have been accustomed to this sort of treatment, for he speedily lay down and went to sleep, as though satisfied to stay with these new friends. Floods as well as politics, often make strange bed-fellows.

Having brought his party safely through this crisis Max was again busying himself making plane looking toward their future. He knew that the country was so disturbed by the inundation of the river, with its consequent damage to many homes, that they must depend to a great extent on their own efforts in order to reach Carson again. Still it seemed necessary in the start that one of their number should start out to seek help in the way of some conveyance by means of which the girls and Mrs. Jacobus might be taken to Carson, because he and his chums were well able to walk that distance.

On talking this over with the rest, and Shack was invited to join them, much to the secret satisfaction of the "black sheep" of Carson, Max found that they were all opposed to his being the one to go forth. They claimed that he would be needed right along in order to continue the management of affairs.

Of course Shack could not go, because his former bad reputation would serve to set people against him, for the whole country knew of the doings of the gang to which he had belonged; Toby was debarred from serving on account of his infirmity in the line of speech, and so it must lie between Bandy-legs and Steve.

"I'm the one to go, Max," declared the latter, so resolutely that while Bandy-legs had just been about to volunteer, the words died on his lips; for he knew that when Steve really wanted a thing he must have it, or there would be trouble in the camp; so that Bandy-legs, being a wise youth, shrugged his shoulders and yielded the palm.

Once more Max talked it all over with them. They knew next to nothing about the lay of the land around that section, but in a general way that could be figured out; and Steve was cautioned what to avoid in looking for a habitation where he might manage to hire a rig of some sort.

Max even made him a rough map, showing some features of the river bank as it was now constituted, so that the messenger would know where to return if he was fortunate enough to secure help.

"If we're gone from here," said Max, in conclusion, "we'll manage to leave such a plain trail after us that you can follow as easy as anything."

So Steve went around solemnly shaking hands with every one, though he lingered longest when it came to Bessie; and she must have said something pleasant, for he was smiling broadly as though satisfied when he waved them good-bye, and stick in hand, vanished amidst the trees of the forest.

CHAPTER XIV

UNWELCOME GUESTS

After Steve had been gone for some little time those who had been left in the camp under the forest trees prepared to spend the night as best the conditions allowed.

Fortunately there were enough of the blankets and covers to go around, so that each one would have some protection against the chill of the night. Max had been wise enough to look out for this when skirmishing around in that abandoned cabin belonging to Mrs. Jacobus.

"Will we have to keep any sort of watch, d'ye think, Max?" Bandy-legs asked, after the girls had crawled beneath the rustic shelter, and amid more or less laughter made themselves fairly comfortable.

Max smiled.

"Yes, but that doesn't necessarily mean any of us will have to stay awake," he went on to say, which remark caused the other to look puzzled until he saw Max nod his head over toward the spot where the ferocious bulldog calmly reposed, with his square head lying between his two forepaws.

"Oh! I see now what you mean," Bandy-legs announced; "and that's where your head was level, Max, though for that matter it always is. Sure he'll be the best sentinel agoing. But then there isn't one chance in a thousand we'll be bothered with visitors, unless of the hungry dog kind."

"That's so," agreed Max, "but you never can tell; and while the roads are all more or less flooded, and even the railroad blocked, tramps are apt to bob up in places where they've never been known before. We'll be keeping our fire going all night, you know, and that would be a signal to any one passing."

The four boys fixed themselves so that they really surrounded the shelter; constructed of boards and branches, in which the girls were snugly settled down. Max had told Mazie they meant to do this, for he felt that the fact would add more or less to the peace of mind of those whom they were protecting.

"Better get settled, you fellows," Max told the others, "and after that I'll attend to the fire so it'll keep burning a long time. Shack, what's that rag around your finger for? I hope now you didn't get bitten by one of the dogs when we had our row, because that might turn out to be a bad job."

"Oh! shucks, that ain't nawthin' much," Shack replied, with scorn; "I on'y knocked me fin against a tree when I was smackin' that setter a whack. He ducked too quick for me, yuh see, an' I lost him, worse luck; but second time I gives him a poke that made him howl like fits."

It apparently pleased Shack considerably to have Max notice that he had his finger bound up in part of a much soiled handkerchief. And by now even Bandy-legs seemed to have accepted the other as a companion in arms, whom the fortunes of war had thrown into their society.

Max took a look around before finally lying down. He saw that clouds still obscured the sky, but at least it was not raining, and there seemed a fair chance that the anticipated renewal of the storm would not materialize.

There must have been thousands of anxious eyes besides those of Max Hastings surveying that overcast sky on this particular night, because so much depended on whether the sun shone on the morrow, or another dripping day were ushered in, to add to the floods, and increase the discomfort and money loss.

He knew that the girls must all be dreadfully worried because messages could not be sent to their respective homes, so as to notify their loved ones of their safety; but it could not be helped. When morning came they would do everything in their power to get in touch with civilization, and if the wires were in working order perhaps they might be able to let their people know how wonderfully they had come out of the turmoil and peril.

When Max told the others there was always a possibility that the light of their fire would draw attention to the camp, he hardly dreamed how true his words would prove; yet such was the case.

He had managed to get to sleep himself, having found a fairly comfortable position where he could lie wrapped in his blanket, when the growling of the tied bulldog aroused him. As he sat up he saw that Bose was on his bowed feet, and continuing to growl savagely.

"Keep quiet there, you ugly sinner!" grumbled a voice close to Max, and which he recognized as belonging to Bandy-legs; "ain't you meanin' to let a feller have any sleep at all to-night? Whatever do you want to growl that way? Wait till breakfast time and you'll get another feed."

"There's somebody coming!" said Max, quietly, "and the dog has sensed them."

"Gee whiz! then he's an all right sentry after all, ain't he?" exclaimed Bandy-legs, immediately sitting up.

Toby had also been aroused, as was also Shack; and the four boys gained their feet at almost the same time.

"Wonder who it is?" Bandy-legs was speculating, even as he leaned over so as to pick up his war club.

"B-b-bet you it's Steve c-c-coming back!" ventured Toby, and he voiced what was in the mind of Max just then.

"There's two on 'em!" declared Shack Beggs joining in with the talk; "yuh c'n see 'em over there aheadin' this way!"

Max was glad that he had not thought to return the little weapon entrusted to his care by Mrs. Jacobus. He allowed his hand to pass back to the rear pocket in which it reposed, and the very feel of the steel seemed to give him a sense of security.

All of them could easily see the advancing figures now. The closer they came to the circle of firelight the stronger did the convictions of Max become that the campers were in for another unpleasant experience.

First it had been half-starved dogs hunting in a pack, having gone back to the primeval habits of their wolfish ancestors; and now it looked as though they were about to suffer from an invasion of tramps.

The two men who came boldly forward certainly had a hobo look. Their clothes were tattered and torn, as though they might only be fit for scarecrows in the newly planted corn field; while their faces were unkempt with beards of a week's growth; which helped to make them look uglier than might otherwise have been the case.

"Whew! they look hungry enough to eat us out of house and home," Bandy-legs was muttering, as he saw the pair pushing forward; and seemingly sniffing the air after the manner of those who have not broken their fast for many hours.

If Max could feel sorry for a dog that needed food he certainly would not think of allowing human beings to go without refreshments as long as they had enough and to spare. So that already his mind was made up not to refuse should the tramps put in a pitiful plea for assistance.

Of course their coming would make it necessary for the boys to give up thoughts of finding any further rest; because it would hardly be wise to allow the camp to remain unguarded with such tough looking customers around.

The men were scrutinizing the campers closely as they came up. Max saw one of them turn to the other and say something; just what it was he did not know; but he rather fancied it might have been along the order of calling his attention to the fact that they had only "kids" to deal with.

"Hello! boys!" the foremost of the men called out as he strode into the circle of light; "seen your fire when we was makin' our way through these here old woods, and allowed that p'raps we might get a bite to eat if we came over. Hain't had nawthin' since mornin', and we're nigh famished, that's straight goods; ain't it, Bill?"

"I'm that near gone I could chaw on a dog biscuit and like it!" grumbled the shorter man.

"This flood's knocked honest laborers out of their jobs right along, boys," the taller hobo continued, unable to repress a slight grin as he spoke, for he must have been pretty positive that he had not deceived the young fellows by such an absurd suggestion; "and we're trying to git acrost country so's to find work in another quarry. If now youse could only let us have a snack it'd be doin' a real kindness, and we'd thank you straight; wouldn't we, Bill?"

"Sure thing, Pepper, we would; got to have somethin', or we'll cave in; and like enough you wouldn't want our spooks to come back and ha'nt ye allers, kids. So here's hopin' ye'll give us a hand-out without more parleyin'."

Max did not fancy the manner of the two men. It smacked of a demand rather than a request for assistance; as though they would not take no for an answer, but might be expected to make trouble if refused.

While something within him rebelled against being compelled to accede, at the same time Max was ready to make allowances. He fancied that when men were really very hungry they might be excused for showing an irritable disposition. On that account then he repressed his desire to speak sharply.

"You've struck a party of flood sufferers, and we're not overly well supplied with grub," Max went on to say; "but I guess we can spare you something to keep the wolf from the door. Just sit down there, and we'll cook you a little supper, though you might call it breakfast, because it must be long after midnight."

The men exchanged low words, and then sat down. Max noticed that they seemed to choose their places as with some motive in view, and he did not like it at all. He even saw them glance toward the shelter shack, as if wondering what might be inside, for the girls were awake, and low whispering could be heard within.

The food had been taken from the shack and hung from the limb of a tree, where it would be safe from any prowling animal; so that Max did not have to disturb the inmates of the rude shelter when he wished to cut some more of the ham, and get the coffee in the pot.

It was a strange experience, this cooking a supper at such an hour of the night for a pair of ugly-looking trampish customers; but Max was so thankful over the wonderful run of good luck that had followed himself and chums that he felt willing to put himself to considerable trouble in order to assist any other sufferer. In times like that it was really a duty they owed to the community to stretch out a helping hand to every one who professed to be in need.

Bandy-legs, Toby and Shack Beggs wanted to assist as best they could, but probably their main object was to keep moving, and in this way find chances for the exchange of a few sentences half under their breath, when it happened that their heads came close together.

"Look like tough nuts to me!" Bandy-legs told Max the first opportunity he had, as he poked the fire and induced it to burn more brightly.

"That's right," replied Max, in the same cautious manner; "so keep your eyes about you all the while; and be ready to swing your club if it turns out to be necessary."

"Bet you I will, Max!" muttered the other; "I wonder now if they've got any gun between 'em? Gosh! if we ain't meetin' up with a trail of happenings these days and nights! I say, Max?"

"What is it, Bandy-legs?"

"Hope now you ain't never give that jolly little automatic back to the lady?" continued Bandy-legs, eagerly.

"I've still got it handy, make your mind easy on that score," was what the other told him, and Bandy-legs evidently breathed considerably easier on that account.

"Keep shy of 'em when you go to hand over the grub, Max; 'cause I wouldn't put it past that crowd to try and grab you. They just understand that you're the boss of this camp, and if they could only get their hands on you it'd be easy to make the rest of us kowtow to 'em."

"You've got a knife in your pocket, haven't you?" asked Max, as he leaned over to give the fryingpan another little shove, as though wishing to hurry matters along, because the two intruders were hungrily watching the preparation of the midnight meal, and looking as though they could hardly wait for the call.

"Yes, I always carry one, you know, Max."

"Pretty good edge, has it?" pursued the other.

"Sharp as a razor, right now," was Bandy-legs' assurance.

"All right, then," Max told him; "keep staying close to where the dog's tied, and if you hear me shout out to you, draw your knife blade across the rope when he's drawn it taut. I've got an idea he'll look on all of us as friends, and make for one of the men like a flash!"

"Fine! I'll do it, see if I don't!"

"Well, get away now, and take up your station," cautioned Max. "Keep watching how they act, but don't give it away that you're looking too close. That's all!"

Upon that Bandy-legs moved off. Presently he had passed over to where Bose was tied to the tree. The bulldog had ceased to strain at his leash. He lay again with his massive square head resting on his forepaws, a favorite attitude with him; and his bulging eyes seemed to be fixed on the two newcomers. Evidently he did not trust the ragged tramps, but as his protectors seemed to be granting them the privileges of the camp, far be it from him to interfere; all the same he was going to watch them closely.

Max was becoming more and more disturbed. From the manner of the men he felt positive that they would refuse to quietly quit the camp after they had been duly fed. That would mean they must be told to go away, and such an order coming from mere boys would be apt to arouse their evil natures so that trouble must ensue.

While he was finishing the cooking of the ham, with the coffee boiling merrily near by on a stone that lay close to the fire, Shack came up with some more fuel. As there was really no need for additional wood Max understood that the other wished to get close enough to him to say something; so he managed things in a way calculated to bring this about.

Sure enough Shack quickly lowered his head as he pushed a stick into the fire, and Max heard his whisper, which naturally gave him something of a thrill.

"Jailbirds, I sure reckons they be!" was what Shack said.

"What makes you think so?" asked Max.

"Both got on ole cloes took from scarecrows in the medders; and then if yuh looks right sharp at the left wrist o' ther short coon yuh kin see he's awearin' a steel bracelet. Been handcuffed tuh a sheriff, likely, an' broke away. They'll like as not try tuh run the camp arter they gits filled up. Yuh wanter keep shy o' lettin' 'em git hold o' yuh, Max. They'll be a reg'lar mixup hereabouts if they tries that same on."

And this information from Shack, who must know what he was talking about, was enough to make Max draw his breath uneasily.

CHAPTER XV

BOSE PAYS FOR HIS BOARD

When he had set the supper on the ground, and then backed away, Max was simply taking precautions. Doubtless the men noticed what he did, and knew from this that he did not trust their professions of friendliness; for they exchanged further talk in low words that were not intelligible to any of the boys.

The girls, unable to longer restrain their natural curiosity, had thrust their heads from the shelter to see what it all meant; and the men must have seen them, though they were savagely attacking the food that had been placed before them.

It was astonishing how quickly they cleared their pannikins of the cooked ham and potatoes, as well as gobbled what crackers Max had been able to spare. Each swallowed two cups of scalding coffee without a wink.

When the entire amount of food had been made to vanish as though struck by a cyclone, Max expected there would be something doing. He knew the crisis was close at hand, and his cough warned the others to be on the alert. Bandy-legs shuffled a little nearer the recumbent bulldog, and the hand he held behind him really clutched his open knife, with the keen blade ready to do its duty by that rope. Shack and Toby sat close together. They had their hands clasped around their knee but were prepared to bound to their feet like a flash; and close beside them lay their war clubs "ready for business at the old stand," as Toby would have said had he been given the chance to express his opinion.

The men were now very close to the end of their meal. It had been a fairly bountiful spread, considering the conditions, but from the rapidity with which those two unwelcome guests caused it to vanish it looked as though they might still be far from satisfied.

The taller one began to crane his neck after the manner of a diner in a restaurant looking to see whether the next course was on the way or not.

"Hopes as how that ain't all you means to hand out, younker?" he went on to say, with a little menace in his manner that did not seem to be just the right thing for one to display who had been treated so well.

"As our stock of food isn't so very large, and we don't know just how long we may have to camp out, it's all we can spare just now," replied Max, in as amiable a tone as he could command.

After all it was a mistake to suppose that men like these desperate rascals would allow themselves to feel anything like gratitude. Their instincts were brutal to the core, and they only knew the law of force. These boys and girls had plenty to eat, and they were far from satisfied. If further food was not forthcoming through voluntary means, they would just have to take things as they pleased. They could have nothing to fear from interruptions, in this lonely neighborhood; and as for these four half-grown boys putting up a successful fight against two such hardened characters as they were, was an absurdity that they did not allow to make any impression on them.

Still the taller man did not want to rush things too fast. There was something about the cool manner of Max Hastings that warned him the conquest might not be the easy task they thought, he may have sensed the fact that the young leader of the camping party was not an ordinary boy; and then too Shack Beggs had a husky sort of look, as though he knew pretty well how to take care of himself.

The bulldog had kept so quiet all this time that the men did not pay much attention to him, lying there peacefully. They probably calculated that if things came down to an actual show of hands it would mean two boys apiece; and surely they should be equal to overcoming such opposition.

"Hain't that same kinder rough on us, young feller?" demanded the hobo or escaped jailbird, whichever the taller man might be. "Wot yer gives us only makes us hungrier'n 'ever. Wisht you'd look 'round an' see if yer cain't skeer up somethin' more in the line o' grub. Then we'll stretch out here nigh yer fire, an' git some sleep, 'cause we needs the same right bad."

"You've had all we can let go," said Max; "and as your room is better than your company, perhaps you'll feel like moving on somewhere else for the night. If it happens that you've no matches to make a fire to keep warm by, there's part of a box for you," and he coolly tossed a safety-match box toward the taller man, one of a number he had found on a shelf in Mrs. Jacobus' cabin.

Somehow his defiant words caused the men to turn and look dubiously at each other. They hardly knew what to expect. Could that shack shelter several men besides the girls whose frightened faces they could see peeping out? There did not seem to be any chance of that being the case, both decided immediately. After exchanging a few muttered sentences the two men began to slowly gain their feet.

Shack Beggs and Toby also scrambled erect, holding their cudgels behind them prepared for work. Those men looked dangerous; they would not be willing to leave that comfortable camp at the word of a boy, a mere stripling, at least not until the conditions began to appear more threatening than at present.

Max was watching their every action. He had nerved himself for the crisis, and did not mean to be caught napping. Should either of the men show a sudden disposition to leap toward them Max was ready to produce his weapon, and threaten dire consequences. The hand that had not quivered when that huge mastiff was in the act of attacking them would not be apt to betray Max now, as these rascals would discover to their cost.

"That's kind in yer, kid, amakin' us a present o' matches when we ain't got nary a one," remarked the spokesman of the pair, as he turned toward Max, and took a step that way.

"Hold on, don't come any closer!" warned the boy, threateningly.

"What's the matter with yer?" snarled the man, suddenly dropping the mask that he had been figuratively wearing while using soft words.

The bulldog must have seen that the danger line had been reached, for he was erect again, and pulling ferociously at his tether, gnashing his ugly white teeth together with an ominous sound, and showing his red open mouth.

"Just what I said before," returned Max, steadily; "you came here without any invitation from us. We've warmed you, and fed you the best we could afford, and now we tell you that we want your room a heap more than your company. That's plain enough English, isn't it, Mister, or do you want me to tell you to clear out?"

The taller man laughed, but it was a very unpleasant sort of a laugh, which must have made the listening girls shiver with dread of what might be coming when those two burly men flung themselves at the boys in the attempt to capture the camp with its spoils.

"Oh! so that's the way the thing runs, is it, kid?" sneered the man; and then changing his manner again he went on to demand harshly: "What if we don't mean to clear out? Supposin' we takes a notion this here is comfy enough fur two ducks that'd like to stay to breakfast, and share yer stock o' grub? What'd ye do 'bout that, younker?"

He took another forward step, and from his aggressive manner it was plain to be seen that he meant to attack them speedily. Max waited no longer. He did not want matters to work along until they reached the breaking point, for that would mean a nasty fight; and while he and his chums would undoubtedly come out of this first-best there must be some bruises received, and perhaps blood might have to be shed. So he concluded to stop things where they were.

Accordingly he brought his hand to the front and made so as to let them see he was armed. As the hobo did not advance any further it looked as though he may have taken warning; the sight of that up-to-date weapon was enough to make any one pause when about to precipitate trouble, for it could be fired as fast as Max was able to press the trigger.

"Bandy-legs!" snapped Max.

"Here!" answered the one addressed.

"Have you got your knife laid on the rope?" continued the leader of the camp.

"You just bet I have, and when you say the word he's goin' to jump for that biggest feller's throat like a cyclone; ain't you, Bose?" turning toward the dog.

The ugly looking bulldog gave a yawp that may have been intended for an affirmative answer; and his appearance was so very fierce that it helped the hobo make up his mind he did not care for any closer acquaintance with such an affectionate beast.

"Hold on there, don't you be in too big a hurry 'bout slittin' that same rope, kid!" he called out, shrinking back a step now, and half raising his hands as if to be in readiness to protect his neck against those shining teeth.

"Then you've changed your mind about wanting to sleep here in this camp, have you?" asked Max, quietly. "We'll allow you to do it on one condition, which is that you let us tie you both up, and hold you here until the sheriff comes to-morrow."

From these words it became apparent to the men that the fact of one of them was wearing a broken handcuff must have been discovered by the boys. They looked as black as a thunder cloud, but realized that they were up against a blank wall.

"Excuse us 'bout that same, kid," the taller man said, bitterly; "we'd rather take the matches an' go to make a camp somewhere else, where we won't bother youse any. But p'raps ye'll be sorry fur actin' like that by us, won't he, Bill?"

"He will, if ever I has anythin' tuh say 'bout it," growled the shorter rascal, shaking his bullet-shaped head, which the boys now saw had been closely shaven, which would indicate that he must in truth be some escaped convict.

"We're waiting for you to move along," remarked Max. "Don't bother thanking us for the little food we had to spare you. It may keep you from starvation, anyway. And see here, if so much as a single stone comes into this camp after you've gone I give you my word we'll cut that rope, and start the dog after you. Now just suit yourselves about that!"

The men gave one last uneasy look at the bulldog, and as though he knew he was in the spotlight just then Bose growled more fearfully than ever, and showed still more of his spotted throat, and red distended jaws, with their attendant white, cruel looking fangs.

It was enough. The taller man shook his head dismally as though, knowing that neither of them possessed the first weapon, he judged it would be something bordering on suicide to provoke that fierce beast to extreme measures.

"There'll be no stone throwin', make yer mind easy on that score, younker," he told Max, between his teeth; "but if ever we should happen to meet up with you er any o' yer crowd agin, look out, that's all! Kim erlong, Bill, we quits cold right here, see?"

With that they stalked moodily away, and the boys seemed able to draw freer breaths after their departure. Max stood ready to carry out his threat should the men attempt to bombard the camp with stones, and for some little time he kept Bandy-legs standing there, knife in hand, ready to sever the rope that kept Bose from his liberty.

There was no need, it turned out. The two men had realized that they were in no condition to carry matters to a point of open hostilities with those who had fed them and given them a helping hand; and perhaps that vague threat of detaining them there until the coming of the officers may have added to their desire to "shake the dust of that region from their shoes," as Bandy-legs expressed it, although Toby told him he would have a pretty hard time finding anything like dust in those days of rain-storms and floods.

It took a long time to reassure the girls, and coax them to try and sleep again. As for Max he was determined to keep awake, and on guard until dawn arrived; which in fact was exactly what he did.

CHAPTER XVI

AFTER THE FLOOD—CONCLUSION

"Well, it's come morning at last, and for one I'm right glad to see it," and Bandy-legs stretched himself, with numerous yawns, while making this remark.

Max admitted that he felt pretty happy himself to see the day break in the far east, with a prospect for the sun appearing speedily, since the clouds had taken wings and vanished while darkness lay upon the land.

Everybody was soon moving around, and the girls insisted that breakfast should be given over entirely to their charge.

"From what you've told us," Bessie French declared, when there were some plaintive murmurs on the part of Bandy-legs and Max to the effect that they wished to save their guests from all hard work, "we expect that you find plenty of times to do all the cooking that's good for you. Now it isn't often that you have girls in camp to show you what they know about these things; so I think you'd better tell us to do just as we feel like; and that's going to be take charge of the meals as long as we're together."

Of course secretly Max and Bandy-legs were just as well pleased as anything could be over this dictum from the fair ones; they simply wanted to do their duty, and show that they meant right.

Well, that breakfast was certainly the finest the boys had ever eaten while in the woods at any time; and they voted the cooks a great success.

"We'd be happy to have you with us always, when the camping fever came along," Bandy-legs informed them, as he came in for his third helping; "though of course that would be impossible, because we sometimes get away off out of touch with everything, and girls couldn't stand what we put up with. Besides, I don't believe your folks would let you try it. So we'll always have, to remember this time when we get our grits burned, or, something else goes wrong, as it nearly always does when I'm trying to play chef."

After the meal was over they held a council of war to decide upon their next move. It seemed folly to stay there doing nothing to better their condition; and that sort of thing did not correspond with the habits of Max, who believed in getting out and hustling for business, rather than wait for it to come to him.

"We'll get our stuff together, such as we might need in case we do have to stay another night in the forest," he told them in conclusion, when every one had been heard, and it was decided to make a start; "and then head in a certain direction that I told Steve I thought would take him to a road marked on my rough map. If we're real lucky we may even meet Steve headed for this place, with some sort of vehicle that will carry the whole crowd."

No one appeared very enthusiastic, for truth to tell it was not at all unpleasant camping in this way; and only for the fact that they knew their folks would surely be dreadfully worried concerning them the girls secretly confessed to one another that they might have wished the experience to be indefinitely prolonged.

"I'll never forget that cute little shelter," Mazie told Max, as they found themselves about ready to say good-bye to their night's encampment; "and although we did have a bad scare when those two tramps came around, I think I slept almost as well as I should have done at my own home. That's because we all felt such confidence in our guardians. Now, don't get conceited, and believe we think you're perfect, because boys have lots of faults, the same as girls."

"I wonder what became of those two poor fellows?" mused Bessie, who still believed that the men were just ordinary, lazy, good-for-nothing hoboes, with a dislike for hard work, and resting under the conviction that the world owed them a living; for the boys had decided that there was no use telling them about the broken handcuff they had noticed on the wrist of the smaller scamp.

"I wouldn't be surprised if they were miles away from here by now," said Max, with a knowing wink toward Toby, who chanced to be standing near.

"Then they're more active than most tramps I've seen appeared to be," remarked Bessie; "but I do hope we meet Steve coming with some sort of conveyance, because twenty miles over poor roads fills me with horror, though I'll try the best I know how to keep up with the rest of you. Think of poor little Mabel, though; she would be tired before we had gone three miles."

"Never fear but what we'll get hold of some sort of vehicle, sooner or later," Max assured her; "when we strike the road we are bound to run across farms occasionally; and surely they will not all have been deserted. Some of them must be on high land, and safe from the floods."

It was in this spirit that they said good-bye to the pleasant camp, and turned their backs upon the modest but serviceable shack.

"I honestly believe it would shed rain like the back of a duck," Bandy-legs declared, proudly, as though satisfied to know that he had had a hand in building the shelter.

"But we're all glad it wasn't put to the test," Mazie observed, as she looked up at the clear sky with the greatest of pleasure.

It may not have mattered so much to the boys whether or not the rains had stopped for good, but they could understand that there were hosts of people who would be mighty thankful the morning had broken so promising, for if clear weather prevailed the floods would of course have a chance to go down.

Max had laid out his plans as well as he could, on the preceding night, so that he was prepared to move right along the line of least resistance; that is, from the conformation of the country, as marked upon the little map he had drawn of the neighboring region, he meant to select a route that would keep them away from the lowlands, now flooded.

They did not find any great difficulty in making fair progress, although the little lame girl had to be assisted often. She was very brave, however, and anxious to prove that she must not be looked on as helpless.

Inside of an hour they had come upon a road, just as Max had figured would be the case. So far nothing had been seen of Steve, though according to promise they were careful to leave a broad trail behind them, so that if he should visit the camp after their departure he would find no difficulty about following in their wake.

If Steve had faithfully carried out the directions given him, Max knew that he certainly must have reached this same road, and possibly not far from the point at which they too struck it. As he walked along Max was keeping a bright lookout for certain signs which he had arranged Steve should leave on the right-hand side of the hill road to tell them he had been there.

These he discovered inside of ten minutes after they started to travel along the highway, which was in fair condition considering the bad weather. A branch had been partly broken, and as it lay seemed to point ahead. When a short distance beyond they came upon the same thing repeated, there no longer remained the slightest doubt but what it was the work of their absent chum.

Max explained all these things to the girls, partly to cheer them up; and then again because he knew Bessie would be interested in everything that Steve did.

After that they all watched the road at every bend, and hope kept surging up in their hearts as they fancied they heard the distant sound of wheels. What if disappointments came many times, they knew that Steve must be ahead somewhere, and would exhaust every device in the endeavor to accomplish the more important part of his duty.

Just about an hour afterwards they all caught the unmistakable sound of wheels, and then came a well known voice calling to the horses to "get busy"; after which a big hay-rick turned the bend a little way ahead, with

Steve wielding the whip, and a boy perched on the seat alongside him, possibly to bring back the rig after they were through with it.

Loud were the cheers that went up, and no one shouted with more vim than Shack Beggs, who seemed to have gradually come to believe that from this time on there was no longer going to be anything in the shape of a gulf between him and Max, as well as the other chums. He had been through peril in their company, and there is nothing in the wide world that draws people closer together than sharing common dangers.

So the hay-rick was turned around, and the girls made as comfortable as could be done. The boys managed to perch almost anywhere, and were as merry as though they had not a care or a worry in the world.

"Can we make Carson in a day?" Bessie demanded, when the two horses toiled slowly up a rather steep hill.

"I think we will," Max assured her; "if we're lucky, and don't get stalled by some washed-out bridge. But at the worst we ought to get where we can use the wires to send the news home; and find decent shelter to-night, at some farmhouse."

"Now watch us make time!" called out Steve, who was still doing duty as driver, though Bandy-legs and Shack Beggs had both offered to spell him when he got tired.

The grade being down-hill they covered the ground much more rapidly, and amidst more or less shouting the next mile was put behind them.

So they went on until noon came, and Max was of the opinion that more than one-third of their tedious journey had been accomplished. This they learned was a fact when they stopped at a farmhouse, and coaxed the good wife to cook them a glorious dinner, allowing the horses to have a good rest, so that they would be equal to the balance of the day's work.

Max, as usual, improved the opportunity to pick up pointers, and in this way no doubt saved himself and friends more or less useless work; for they heard about a bridge that had been carried away, and were thus enabled to take a branch road that kept to the higher ground.

Once more they were on the move, and headed for home. It was encouraging to learn that the water seemed to be already lowering, as the worst of the freshet had spent its force, and the promised storm had been shunted off in another direction by a fortunate change of wind.

As the afternoon began to draw near its close they found themselves getting in very familiar country, and this told them Carson and home could be only a few miles distant. There was no longer any doubt about making it that evening, though it might be sunset before they arrived at their destination.

Of course this gave the girls more or less happiness, though they protested that they were enjoying themselves hugely. It was far from a comfortable ride at the best, however, and often Bessie and Mazie would gladly get out and walk with some of the boys, while they were climbing hills. This eased the strain on the tired horses, and at the same time gave their own cramped limbs a chance to secure the much needed exercise.

Finally the last hill had been mounted, and there lay Carson bathed in the glow of the setting sun. The boys greeted the welcome sight with lusty cheers, in which two of the girls joined. Mabel did not feel so happy, because she could not forget how her own beloved home had been carried away in the flood; though there was little doubt but that Asa French was able to build him a far better house, and stock his farm afresh, for he had plenty of money out at interest.

The day was over, but the light still remained as the hay-rick, with that little company of boys and girls aboard, reached the streets of Carson. Shouts attested to the interest their coming aroused; for every one knew about the fall of the bridge, and how Max and his comrades were carried away with it. No word having come from them since, of course their families were almost distracted; and it can easily be understood that the warmest kind of welcome awaited all of the castaways on their arrival home.

Carson was already beginning to recover from the shock occasioned by the rising waters. All sorts of "hard luck" stories kept coming to town from neighboring farmers, who were so unfortunate as to live in the lowlands, where the soil's richness had tempted them to make their homes. It seems to always be the case that where danger lurks in the way of floods or volcanic eruptions, there the wonderful productiveness of the soil serves as a lure to tempt people to accept risks. As a rule these folks are able to laugh at their neighbors on the higher lands; but sooner or later there comes a time when things do not look so rosy, and perhaps they lose all their accumulation of years.

Already plans were being discussed to take advantage of the misfortunes that had come upon the community so as to build better. The new bridge would be a beauty, and so staunch that no flood could ever dislodge it. Houses that had been swept away, or ruined in other ways were to be replaced by more commodious and up-to-date buildings, and the new barns would also far outclass those that had gone.

It was perhaps a much needed lesson, and Carson inside of a few years was bound to profit by what at the time had seemed to be the greatest calamity that had ever visited the community.

Max Hastings and his chums would never forget their strange experiences. They had to relate the story many times to the good people of Carson, as well as their schoolmates. That cruise on a floating bridge would go down in the annals of the town as one of the most remarkable events that had ever happened.

Of course Mabel found a chance to communicate with her almost distracted parents and assure them of her safety. None of the three girls suffered in the least as the result of their exposure and privations. They always declared that it had in many ways been the most delightful experience in their lives; and whenever this was said in the presence of

Steve or Max of course those boys smiled contentedly, because they took it as a compliment that Mazie and Bessie considered camping in their company, under such discouraging conditions, as a genuine picnic.

It was perhaps a rather remarkable fact that some of Steve's pictures did actually turn out fairly well. He had tried the best he knew how to keep the little camera from being submerged in the water; and while outwardly the leather case had suffered, the films were very little injured.

They were more than glad of this, because it gave them something tangible as a reminder of the eventful trip, and the strange adventures that followed their being kidnapped by the runaway bridge.

Later on that summer, when they had a chance to make a day's tour in an automobile, Max, Steve, Bandy-legs, and Toby invited both Mazie Dunkirk and Bessie French to accompany them; and in fine style they visited along the route of their homeward journey after leaving the camp under the forest trees.

Nothing would satisfy the two girls but that they must leave the car somewhere and foot it through the well remembered aisles of the dense woods until finally they came upon the dear shack where they had spent that never-to-be-forgotten night.

There they cooked dinner, and enjoyed a real picnic. Every little event of that delightful past was gone over again with exactness; and all of them pronounced the day one of the happiest of the calendar. The shack was still in serviceable condition, and the girls were pleased to pretend that they might still have need of a shelter whenever a cloud as big as a boy's pocket appeared in the sky.

Max never learned what became of the two men who had invaded their camp. Doubtless the annals of some penitentiary might disclose the fact that they had escaped from its walls; but whether they were recaptured or not none of the boys ever knew.

Of course Max and his chums were looking forward to other outings when the vacation period came around again; and we trust that it may be our good fortune to be given the privilege of placing before the reader some account of these stirring happenings. Until such time we can only add that Shack Beggs was surely making good, having completely severed his relations with those cronies who had so many times led him along crooked, ways; and whenever Max has the chance he does not hesitate to hold out a friendly hand to the struggling lad, knowing that it is this encouragement on the part of his boy friends that will do more than anything else to plant Shack's feet firmly on solid ground.

9 781836 571759